PUFFIN BOOKS

MIRANDA AND FF

It's the beginning of the summer holidays and Miranda is looking forward to six whole weeks of freedom, doing whatever she likes while her mum is out at work. But Mum has other ideas. Miranda is to spend every weekday with her bad-tempered, cat-loving grandmother and the two of them don't really get on. In fact, the only good thing about staying with Gran is the overgrown garden of the house behind, which has stood empty since the death of the miserly old man who used to live there.

But now it is empty no longer and Miranda becomes firm friends with Eric, whose family have just moved in, and Miranda soon persuades him that there must be treasure hidden somewhere in the house, probably guarded by the old miser's ghost. Eric is convinced that she is right and although he is mainly confined to a wheelchair, this proves no handicap to the great treasure hunt.

Eric desperately wants to leave his special school and join Miranda at Braddon County Juniors (despite Miranda's sworn enemy, the revolting Jason Fowler). In true Miranda style she takes Eric off to meet Mr Forester, her headmaster, at his house. But it looks like their treasure hunt may not have helped their cause.

This terrific sequel to *Only Miranda* continues the inspiring story of this fiercely independent only child.

Tessa Krailing was born in Kent and brought up in Sussex. She worked for the BBC as a TV drama production secretary, and later trained as a teacher. She taught mainly English and Art before turning to full-time writing. She has written radio and TV plays and is a frequent lecturer at Writers' Workshops. She now teaches Creative Writing in the Isle of Wight, where she lives.

Also by Tessa Krailing

ONLY MIRANDA

Miranda and Friends

Tessa Krailing

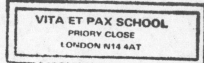

PUFFIN BOOKS

PUFFIN BOOKS

Published by the Penguin Group
Penguin Books Ltd, 27 Wrights Lane, London W8 5TZ, England
Penguin Books USA Inc., 375 Hudson Street, New York, New York 10014, USA
Penguin Books Australia Ltd, Ringwood, Victoria, Australia
Penguin Books Canada Ltd, 10 Alcorn Avenue, Toronto, Ontario, Canada M4V 3B2
Penguin Books (NZ) Ltd, 182–190 Wairau Road, Auckland 10, New Zealand

Penguin Books Ltd, Registered Offices: Harmondsworth, Middlesex, England

First published by Hamish Hamilton 1991
Published in Puffin Books 1992
10 9 8 7 6 5 4 3 2 1

Text copyright © Tessa Krailing, 1991
All rights reserved

The moral right of the author has been asserted

Printed in England by Clays Ltd, St Ives plc

For Linda, Diana and Anne

Contents

1

Come-as-you-please Day

'Miranda Jones,' Mrs Crampton said, 'you are unique.'

Miranda wasn't sure if unique was a good thing or a bad thing to be, so she made her face blank. This wasn't easy if you had a face like Miranda's, which was usually round and smiling or occasionally round and scowling, depending on what kind of a mood she was in.

'I know that today is Come-as-you-please Day,' Mrs Crampton went on, 'and you can wear whatever you wish. But what on earth gave you the idea to come dressed like *that*?'

Miranda thought the answer to this question was obvious. But Mrs Crampton seemed to want her to say it aloud, so she did.

'Because this is what pleases me,' she said.

Jason Fowler groaned and said, 'Typical Miranda!'

The rest of Class 4C grinned. Most of them were celebrating Come-as-you-please Day, which was also the last day of term, by wearing jeans and their favourite T-shirts. Jason's had DENNIS THE MENACE printed across the front. Chrissie Simpson, Miranda's best friend, was wearing her new cotton skirt, dazzlingly patterned in red and yellow, yet Mrs Crampton hadn't even blinked. She had shown surprise only at what Miranda was wearing.

Miranda had come in her pyjamas.

Mind you, they weren't just any old pyjamas. These were World Wide Fund for Nature pyjamas, with a large picture of a panda across the top. Miranda had always thought it a pity that no one ever saw them except Mum, so Come-as-you-please Day seemed too good an opportunity to miss. She hadn't expected anyone to be surprised.

'Tell me,' Mrs Crampton said, 'did you walk to school dressed like that?'

Miranda thought this was an even odder question. 'No, I wore my dressing-gown.'

The other kids giggled behind their hands.

Mrs Crampton looked puzzled. 'And your mother let you?'

'She'd already left for work.'

'So she doesn't know?'

'Well, no,' Miranda admitted. 'But even if she did she wouldn't mind. I'm sure she wouldn't.'

'Hmm,' Mrs Crampton said.

Miranda felt a pang of doubt. Mrs Crampton and her mother were quite good friends. They called each other Pam and Anne. Next time they met Pam Crampton would almost certainly mention Miranda's Come-as-you-please outfit to Anne Jones. Then Anne Jones (alias Mum) would come home and say 'Honestly, Miranda!', and Miranda would feel guilty without really knowing why.

Because she still couldn't see what was so shocking about coming to school in her pyjamas.

At breaktime Maxine Dobbs said she thought the panda was ace. This made Miranda feel better, since Maxine was easily the most popular girl in the class. But when she went into the playground to practise skipping with Chrissie, Jason Fowler called out, 'Just going to bed, then?'

Miranda ignored him.

'Tired, are you?' he persisted. 'Don't let us keep you up.' And he pursued her all round the playground, making loud snoring and honking noises.

Eventually Miranda could bear it no longer. She raised her voice and said, 'Don't look now, Chrissie, but I think we're being followed by a pig.'

Insulted, Jason demanded, 'Who are you calling a pig?'

Miranda pretended to be surprised. 'Oh, it's Jason. Funny, you sounded just like a pig, honking like that.'

Jason honked again, this time with rage.

Chrissie tugged at her arm. 'Come on, don't start fighting with him. He's too big. You know he always wins.'

'I wasn't fighting,' Miranda protested, as she let herself be dragged away. When they were safely out of earshot she giggled and said, 'But he is a bit like a pig. He has little pink piggy eyes and a nose like a snout. All he needs is a curly tail . . .'

They both collapsed with laughter.

As it was the last day of term, going-home time came earlier than usual, which meant that her mother couldn't meet her from school. Mum had only recently started work as a cab driver, which suited her far better than the stuffy old desk job she'd had before, but her shift didn't finish until 2.30 pm. That's why it had been arranged for Miranda to have a lift home with Chrissie.

Mrs Simpson, Chrissie's stepmother, looked surprised when Miranda climbed into the car wearing a quilted dressing-gown, but she only said, 'Well, that's the summer term over. And tomorrow we're off to Australia for six weeks.'

Miranda was shocked. She had known that Chrissie was going away, of course, but hadn't realised it was for the entire summer holiday.

Chrissie screwed round in the seat to look at her. 'I'll send you a postcard.'

'Thanks,' Miranda said, frowning.

'In fact I'll send two postcards,' Chrissie promised, 'to make up for you not going on holiday. It must be awful having to stay here in boring old Braddon.'

Miranda said nothing, but her frown grew deeper. She had only known Chrissie a few weeks, since coming to Braddon County Junior School in the middle of the summer term, and at first she hadn't liked her at all. But then they had become friends and now she found she hated the idea of Chrissie going away. Especially to Australia, which was on the other side of the world. And for *six whole weeks*. She would miss her terribly.

The car stopped in the High Street to let her out. She muttered, 'Thanks for the lift. Have a nice time in

Australia,' and shot across the pavement quickly before the afternoon shoppers had time to notice what she was wearing.

2

Do-as-you-please

Miranda called first at The Jade Dragon to collect the key of the flat from Mr Wing. She often thought that she and Mum must be the luckiest people in the world, living over a takeaway, because even though they couldn't often afford to buy a Chinese meal the smells that came wafting up the stairs were heavenly.

Mr Wing's round pale face, like a full winter's moon, showed no surprise at seeing her in her dressing-gown. He gave her the key and asked, as he usually did, what kind of a day she had had.

'I'm not sure,' Miranda said. 'Mrs Crampton called me unique.'

'She spoke the truth,' Mr Wing said. 'You *are* unique.'

'But is it a good thing to be, that's what I'm not sure about?'

'Oh, definitely good. It means you're the one and only of your kind. In other words, Miss Jones, there's nobody else quite like you in the world.'

Miranda thought about this. It was true that she was the one and only, in the sense that she had no brothers and sisters. Sometimes she wished she had, but then again she was often glad she hadn't. The flat had only one bedroom, which meant that Mum had to sleep on a sofa-bed in the living-room. It would be far too crowded if they were a large family.

On the other hand, it would be nice to have company, especially during the holidays.

She said, 'There's something else. Chrissie Simpson's going to Australia tomorrow with her family. That means I shan't have anyone to play with.'

'So?' Mr Wing looked unimpressed.

'So I'm going to get pretty bored, being by myself all day.'

Mr Wing sighed. 'Tell me, Miss Jones, do you consider yourself to be a boring person?'

This question seemed to Miranda by far the oddest she'd been asked all day. 'Of course not,' she said.

'In that case, how can you possibly be bored by your own company? Confucius says that the man who hates being alone is the man who is most often alone, for how can he expect others to like him if he doesn't like himself?'

Confucius, Miranda knew, had lived in China a long time ago and said a lot of wise things, according to Mr Wing. And this, now she thought about it, was extremely wise. Six weeks of her own company meant she could do whatever she liked, whether it was writing poetry or eating chicken chow mein with her fingers. Mum wouldn't know, because she'd be out at work. Miranda would be able to please herself day after day after day . . .

As she turned to go, Mr Wing said, 'You'd better

tell your mother, I heard today we've got a new landlord. The whole block's been sold – shops, flats, everything. No one's told us yet officially, but it seems quite certain.'

Miranda promised to pass on the message and climbed the steep, narrow staircase to the flat.

The first thing she did was to change into her jeans and her favourite tunic top, in case Mum should come home early and catch her in her pyjamas. Then she sat down on the bed with her notebook to compose an end-of-term poem. It went like this:

No mor maths, no mor ~~skool~~ ~~shool~~ scool food.
No mor Jayson being rood.
No mor pleezing Missis C.
Six hole weeks of pleezing ME!

No doubt about it, she was getting better and better at writing poetry. This one actually rhymed.

She heard her mother's key in the lock and went to meet her.

Mum looked exhausted. She collapsed into the nearest chair and said, 'Sorry I'm late, but the traffic's foul. And my last fare was in a hurry to catch a train and had loads of luggage.' She kicked off her shoes. 'How was your day, pet?'

'Okay,' Miranda said guardedly. 'Mr Wing gave me a message. He said to tell you we've got a new landlord.'

'I heard that too.' Mum's eyelids began to droop as if she couldn't stay awake another minute. 'Let's hope he doesn't want to put the rent up.'

Miranda was alarmed. If the new landlord put up

the rent they might not be able to pay it and then they'd have to go back to living with Gran. They had lived with Gran for a whole month when they first came to Braddon and Miranda had hated every minute. Gran had a very sharp tongue and her house was dark and full of spiders.

'Do you think he will?' she asked anxiously.

Mum opened her eyes and smiled. 'No, I was joking. He can't put up the rent for at least a year, it's in the terms of our lease. Don't look so worried, we're quite safe.'

Miranda breathed a sigh of relief. Her spirits rose immediately. 'Today was the last day of term,' she reminded her mother. 'Tomorrow I'm on holiday.'

'I realise that.' Mum's eyelids began to droop again. 'It's all right, I've made arrangements.'

Miranda felt a pang of alarm. 'Arrangements?'

'You're going to your grandmother's. Not to stay, of course. You'll come home every evening, just as if you were at school. But you'll be spending each day over at Gran's house.'

Miranda's pang grew to a full-scale red alert. 'I'd rather stay here.'

Mum opened her eyes again, wide. 'Don't be silly, you can't possibly stay here on your own. What on earth would you do with yourself?'

'I'll be okay,' Miranda assured her. 'I'm not a boring person, you know.'

Mum sighed. 'Yes, I do know. And that's exactly why you're going to your grandmother's. It's no use arguing with me, Miranda. My mind's made up.'

3

Africa

Now, grandmothers in books are usually sweet old ladies with snow-white hair and rosy cheeks. They sit in rocking-chairs, knitting socks, and keep jars of mint humbugs in the sideboard to give to visiting grandchildren. And they tell stories about the summery days of their girlhood, when the sun always shone and liquorice sticks were two for a penny.

Miranda's grandmother wasn't a bit like that.

She was small and wiry with red frizzy hair that was no longer naturally red, but had to be touched up with stuff from a bottle. She hated cooking and housework and spent most of her time playing Patience. She always wore trousers, usually with a big floppy shirt, and she chain-smoked, even though the doctor had told her that it was bad for her health.

Oh yes, and she bred cats. Grey ones, with tawny eyes, who sat on the path to watch Miranda arrive – in a taxicab driven by her mother – on the first morning of the school holidays.

Gran met them at the front door. Mum said to her, 'You do see how it is, don't you? I couldn't possibly leave her alone in the flat all day.' And Gran nodded grimly, lighting up another cigarette.

'I'll be back to collect her about four,' Mum added.

Miranda felt like a parcel.

She went to see her mother off at the gate. 'Be good,' Mum said. 'Try not to get into any kind of trouble.'

'Some hopes!' Gran called from the doorway. 'Takes after her father, that one.'

This was by far the worst thing about visiting Gran, that she said unkind things about Dad. Okay, so it was true he was in prison for stealing money from his employers. That's why they had come to live in Braddon only two months ago, and why they had stayed with Gran until Mum found the flat over The Jade Dragon. But it wasn't fair, in Miranda's opinion, to keep going on about it.

Mum said to Miranda in a low voice, 'I'm sorry, pet, but this is the only solution I can think of. You do understand, don't you?'

Miranda wanted to point out that she had already come up with a brilliant solution, namely to stay at home and please herself, as Mr Wing had suggested. But her mother looked so unhappy that she decided not to mention it again. Instead she muttered, 'Just don't be late collecting me, that's all.'

'I won't,' Mum promised. 'At least, not if I can help it.' She got into the cab and drove off.

Miranda went indoors. For a moment she and her grandmother stared at each other without speaking. Then Miranda said, 'It's not my fault.'

'No,' Gran agreed.

'I didn't want to come here. I'd have been all right by myself at home, doing as I please.'

'Oh yes? And what's that?'

'Well, er ... writing poetry.' She didn't think it wise to mention eating chow mein with her fingers.

'You can write poetry here, if you want,' Gran said. 'I don't care what you do, as long as you don't get under my feet.'

Miranda hesitated. Her grandmother's house, although larger than the flat, smelt of cats and cigarette smoke. It wasn't at all the right atmosphere for writing poetry. She said, 'I'd sooner play in the garden.'

'Okay,' Gran said with a shrug. 'Suit yourself.'

Gran's garden was pretty dull, being long and thin with untidy flower beds down each side and a compost heap at the bottom. But beyond the compost heap was a high brick wall, and on the other side of the wall was Africa.

It wasn't really Africa, of course. In fact it was the neglected garden of a house called The Mount, which had stood empty now for about a year, ever since the old man who lived there had died. But when they had first come to live with Gran, and Miranda discovered what lay beyond the wall, her imagination had swiftly taken flight. The temptation to explore this foreign land had been too great to resist; and each time she explored it she seemed to find something new.

She climbed the wall and sat with her legs dangling over the other side. From here she had a bird's eye view over the rampant, ferny tangle beneath. But as soon as she dropped down from the wall she was in another country. A green, rustling, mysterious place, where the foliage grew higher than her head. Wild creatures lived here, small and scuttling. Grey shadows with tawny eyes stalked silently through the undergrowth, hunting for food.

Africa.

Miranda Jones, conservationist and explorer, hitched up her jeans – she had just made an emergency parachute jump from an airliner with engine trouble – and set off into the interior. Today she would leave the beaten track to explore new territory, where no human being had ever set foot before. It would be risky, of course. Who knew what dangers lay beyond the trailing branches of the willow tree? But Miranda Jones never flinched from danger.

Cautiously she crept forward. A twig snapped beneath her foot and she stood still, holding her breath. Nothing stirred. She crept forward again, bending low beneath a willow branch.

After a few more steps she came to a halt. Something was different. The ground beneath her feet felt squelchy and there was a dampness in the air, a smell of water, the whine of a mosquito.

She was standing at the edge of a swamp. Another two steps and she would have gone right in, up to her armpits in stinking mud. There might even be alligators . . .

Before she had time to check on this her eye was caught by something on the far side of the swamp, a broken-down wooden building with shattered windows and ivy growing over the roof.

A ruined temple!

She started towards it at once, surprised she hadn't discovered it before, especially as there was a path leading right up to it. On her previous expeditions she must have passed close by without even noticing it.

Two steps led up to a shabby green door. At first she thought it was locked, but then she realised it was only stuck. A good hearty heave with her shoulder was all it needed. She half fell through the open doorway.

Inside, the temple was disappointing. No statues. No hidden caskets of gold and silver. Plenty of cobwebs, though, draped over a couple of faded canvas deckchairs, and some rusty old garden tools.

There was also a strong smell of cats.

Holding her nose, Miranda came out again into the fresh air. Well, it hadn't been such a bad expedition. A swamp *and* a ruined temple, all in one day . . .

Then she heard an unexpected noise.

Something was crashing through the undergrowth towards her. Something large and powerful, hacking a path to the temple with what sounded like an axe. Something that moved alarmingly fast . . .

4

Mount House

Miranda began to back through the temple entrance. Best to take cover, hide until the creature had passed. She was just about to close the door when she heard a distant female voice calling, 'Ear – ache!'

Instantly the crashing stopped.

Miranda held her breath.

The voice called again. 'Ear – ache!'

Nothing moved.

Miranda felt as if she were playing that game when somebody shouts 'Freeze' and if you don't freeze immediately you're out. Only this time somebody had shouted 'Earache', which didn't seem to make any kind of sense, but it had exactly the same effect. She dared not move a muscle.

Neither did the creature.

Yet it was still out there, she was sure of it. Somewhere, on the far side of the swamp, a pair of hostile eyes watched her every movement.

Miranda came to a decision. She couldn't stay where she was all afternoon, half in and half out of the temple. Better to make a run for it . . .

She jumped off the step and ran as fast as she could

along the winding path. But she could hear the creature rumbling and crashing behind her. Whichever way she turned it seemed to follow.

And she couldn't find the wall!

This was stupid, she knew perfectly well where the wall was. She had found it easily enough before. Fear was muddling up her sense of direction.

She stopped for a moment, to catch her breath.

The creature stopped too.

She took a step forward.

The creature moved too.

Panicking, Miranda fled down a path choked with brambles. They clawed at her skin and tore her clothes, but she kept on running until, to her relief, she saw the back of Mount House ahead of her.

Then she came to a full stop.

A woman stood in her path, snipping bits off a rose bush with a pair of secateurs. Without looking round, she said, 'This garden is an absolute jungle.'

Miranda said nothing. She already knew it was a jungle. What else would you expect in Africa?

The woman went on, 'I don't believe anyone's pruned these roses for years. It's such a shame.'

Miranda's heartbeat slowed almost to normal. The woman spoke so matter-of-factly that her fears began to seem ridiculous. The creature, whatever it was, wouldn't dare to attack her now. She cleared her throat and said, 'That's because nobody's lived here for a long time.'

The woman swung round at once. 'Good heavens! Who are you?'

'Miranda Jones. My grandmother lives over there, on the other side of the wall.'

The woman nodded. 'She keeps cats.'

It was hard to tell from her voice whether she liked cats or disapproved of them. She looked rather a dreamy person, with large, light blue eyes that seemed ready to start out of her head. Her hair was fair and wispy and her face quite unlined, apart from two deep frown marks between her eyebrows. Miranda thought this probably meant she was short-sighted.

The woman cut another rose and sniffed it. 'They have a lovely smell, these old-fashioned roses. Much nicer than the modern ones.' She added casually, 'Our name is Elderfield, by the way.'

Miranda glanced toward the house. A french window stood open and she could see furniture inside, and some tea chests. 'Did you just move in?' she asked.

'Yes, we did. That's why everything's in such a muddle. I don't know if we'll ever be straight.'

Miranda almost offered to help. She had learned a lot about getting straight when she and her mother moved into the flat. What stopped her was the thought of the creature in the garden. She wouldn't want to risk meeting up with *that* again!

'Tell me,' Mrs Elderfield said, fixing Miranda with her large blue eyes, 'did you see my son?'

'Your son?'

'I seem to have lost him. He went to play in the garden.' She frowned, and the lines between her eyebrows grew even deeper. 'I do hope he's all right.'

Something clicked inside Miranda's brain. 'You can't come to much harm in a garden,' she said.

'I suppose not.' Mrs Elderfield sounded doubtful. 'I thought perhaps you might have met him?'

'No,' Miranda said offhandedly. 'No, I didn't.' She began to move nearer to the house. 'Do you mind if I go back through your side gate? Only it's quite difficult, climbing over that wall.'

Mrs Elderfield nodded. 'You must come again sometime.'

'Uhuh.' Miranda was careful not to commit herself. She might come again, if only to get her own back on Mrs Elderfield's son for giving her such a scare.

On the other hand, she might not.

When she walked through the kitchen door Gran said, 'About time too. Lunch is on the table.'

Lunch was sliced bread and hard butter and even harder cheese. There was a bowl of eating apples but they looked pretty hard too.

'Saints alive!' Gran said, suddenly noticing Miranda's ripped shirt and bramble-scratched arms. 'You haven't been teasing the cats, I hope? I've warned you before, they're not to be trifled with.'

Miranda sat down at the table and helped herself to bread. 'No, it wasn't the cats,' she said. 'I went exploring in next door's garden.'

'It's been sold.'

'Yes, I know.' She gave up trying to spread the butter and took some cheese instead. 'I met the new people. They're called Elderfield.'

'Fancy name,' Gran said with a sniff. 'Well, they'll have a hard job pulling that place into shape again. Old Ebenezer Scrooge let it get into a terrible mess.'

'Was that really his name?' Miranda asked. 'Ebenezer Scrooge?'

'No, it was Joseph Hardcastle. But he was a real old miser, just like Scrooge. Some people say he'd made a fortune in his time, but he died a pauper, so heaven only knows what he did with his money. He certainly never spent any of it on that house.'

'Perhaps he buried it in the garden,' Miranda suggested. 'In an old wooden chest.'

'Could have done. I wouldn't put it past him.'

Miranda gave up trying to eat the bread and cheese and pushed her plate aside. 'Anyway, Mrs Elderfield knows about the cats, but she doesn't seem to mind.'

'Too bad if she does,' Gran said.

'Oh, and she has a son called Earache.'

'Why's he called that?'

Miranda shrugged and bit into an apple. It was as hard as it looked but surprisingly sweet.

'When you've finished eating you'd better get cleaned up,' Gran said. 'Or your mother will have a fit when she sees you.'

Mum came to collect her on the dot of four. She didn't mention the ripped shirt or the scratches on Miranda's arms until they were safely inside the cab, driving home. Then she said wearily, 'Okay, so now tell me what happened.'

Miranda said she had been sitting on the wall at the end of Gran's garden when she fell off, into some

27

brambles. She had been so scared that she ran round the garden, through more brambles, trying to find the way out. It was partly the truth, if not the whole truth.

Mum said, 'Honestly, Miranda!'

For a while they drove in silence, until Mum said, 'Other than that, how was your day?'

Miranda thought for a moment. Then she said, 'Okay.'

'So you won't mind going again tomorrow?'

'No,' she said cautiously. 'No, I won't mind.'

In fact she was already making plans for tomorrow.

5

Earache

Miranda sat astride the wall, waiting and watching. So far there had been no sign of movement in the undergrowth beneath her, but sooner or later, she felt sure, the enemy would appear. Then she would strike – and this time the surprise would all be on *her* side.

Luckily, she had brought her notebook, so she opened it and began composing a poem about Africa.

> Down in the jungel nuthing sters
> No berds sing, no big cat pers
> A dangrus beest is hideing ther
> I wunder if he –

At this point, before she could complete the line with 'knows I'm here', she saw the leaves of a rhododendron bush begin to shake. Seconds later the azalea next to it shivered, even though there was no wind, and there came a faint sqeaking sound, as if something mechanical were passing underneath.

Miranda kept very still.

The squeaking stopped.

In a low, sighing voice Miranda called 'Ear – ache!', just as she had heard Mrs Elderfield call yesterday.

Nothing moved.

She called again, 'Ear – ache!'

A voice from beneath the bushes said, 'Mum?'

Miranda smiled gleefully. He had fallen right into her trap. She spoke in a soft, mysterious whisper. 'Earache, come here. I want to speak to you.'

Silence.

'Come on,' she breathed. 'There's nothing to be afraid of. No one's going to hurt you . . .'

'Who is this?' His voice sounded sharp and irritable.

'I'm a ghost. The ghost of Joseph Ebenezer Hardcastle – '

'Baloney!' The owner of the voice shot out of the bushes and glared up at Miranda. 'Oh, so it's you again. I might have guessed.'

'Earache?' Miranda said uncertainly.

'My name's Eric, dumbo.' He had a long face, with straight brown hair that fell over his forehead, and light blue eyes like Mrs Elderfield's, only not so large. 'I don't need to ask yours, because I already know it.'

'You do?'

'It's Mir – and – a.' He drawled it out in the same way she'd called Ear – ache. 'I heard you tell it to my mother.'

Miranda shifted uncomfortably on the wall. There was a question she just had to ask. She cleared her throat. 'What are you doing in that wheelchair?'

'Sitting down.'

'I can see that,' she snapped back. 'But why?'

'Because I'm tired.' He squinted his eyes to look up at her. 'You realise you're trespassing?'

'No, I'm not. I'm on the wall.'

30

'Your legs are over this side.'

'Legs don't count.'

'Yesterday you were trespassing. You were in our shed.'

'It's only *just* your shed,' Miranda pointed out. 'Nobody lived here before. How was I to know the house had been sold?'

Eric grinned. 'I gave you a fright.'

'No, you didn't.' Honesty made her add, 'Well, only a bit of one.'

'Come off it, you were scared bonkers. That's why you ran.'

'It was the wheelchair,' Miranda said. 'I couldn't think how you were moving so fast. And there was a swishing sound, as if you had a – a sort of knife.'

'My sticks.' He held them up to show her. 'Mostly I use them to push myself along, but they're also useful for clearing a path through the brambles.' He glanced at her arms, still scratched from yesterday. 'Looks like you could have done with them yourself.'

Miranda stuck out her chin. 'Anyway, today it was you who was scared. You thought I was a ghost.'

'Are you nuts? I don't believe in 'em.'

'Well, you soon will.' She jerked her head towards The Mount. 'Didn't you know it was haunted?'

Eric stared at her suspiciously. 'Who says?'

'Everyone.'

In fact Miranda had only just thought of it. But now it seemed obvious. Of course Mount House was haunted. It looked exactly the way a haunted house was supposed to look.

'Oh, yes?' he said sceptically. 'And what kind of a ghost is it supposed to be? Some geezer in a suit of armour? Or a headless woman in white?'

'Don't be stupid. I already told you, it's Joseph Ebenezer Hardcastle.'

'The old bloke who used to live here? Who let the place get into such a mess?'

'That's right. But he had loads of money. My grandmother told me. And when he died they couldn't find it anywhere, so I reckon he must have hidden it.' Suddenly Miranda saw the whole story, clear as day. 'That's why he haunts the place, because he doesn't want anyone to find his treasure.'

'Why not?' Eric demanded. 'It's no use to him now that he's dead.'

'He doesn't want other people to have it. That's what being a miser means, you like to keep things to yourself. Even if you're dead, it makes no difference.' She added, 'We could look for it, if you like.'

'Where?'

She hesitated. Even if she was right – and she was certain now that she was – the treasure chest might be buried anywhere. But they could hardly dig up the whole garden: that wouldn't be practical. 'How about the shed?' she suggested.

Eric shrugged. 'Okay,' he said offhandedly. 'At least it'll be something to do.'

Miranda stuffed the notebook into her pocket and jumped down from the wall.

Eric moved quite fast along the path, knocking aside the brambles with his sticks. He seemed to know the way better than she did, even though he had only just moved into Mount House.

When they came to the shed, which Miranda still liked to think of as a ruined temple, he stopped. 'Wheelchairs don't climb steps,' he said. 'I'll have to get out.'

He swung himself out of the chair, taking his weight on the sticks. His legs were very stiff and straight and seemed to belong to somebody else, a much smaller person. Miranda noticed there were metal bits sticking out from the bottom of his baggy jeans, attached to his boots, and wished she could ask what was wrong with him, but somehow she didn't like to. He'd been snappy enough when she'd asked what he was doing in a wheelchair. She dared not even offer to help him, apart from holding open the door for him to go through.

'Be careful,' she warned. 'Some of the floorboards are rotten.' She followed him in. The door swung to behind them.

'Okay, so where do we start?'

Miranda stared round the shed. If there *was* treasure hidden here it wouldn't be anywhere obvious. 'Under the floor,' she said.

'In that case,' Eric said, 'one of the boards should be loose. All we have to do is find out which one it is.' He began prodding around with his stick.

Miranda got down on her hands and knees, testing the boards with her clenched fist; but, although rotten, they all seemed firmly nailed in place.

Suddenly there was a splintering sound as Eric's

stick found a weak spot. When Miranda went to look she saw that the stick had made a small hole. She stuck two fingers into it and wiggled them around, trying to make it bigger. When this didn't work she put her eye to the hole and peered down.

'There's quite a big gap,' she said. 'If we could only – '

'*Ear – ache . . . !*'

Mrs Elderfield's voice called, as before, from a distance.

Miranda giggled. 'You know, it really does sound like – '

'Sssh!' Eric's face was suddenly fierce.

Puzzled, Miranda said, 'I don't think she'll mind me being here. She said yesterday I could come again – '

'*Shut up!*'

'But – '

'Ear – ache!' This time the voice was much closer. 'Come on, I know you're there somewhere. I can see your chair. Stop playing these silly games.'

Eric's eyes were fixed warningly on Miranda's face. She held her breath, aware that he wasn't playing a game, he was serious. For some reason he didn't want his mother to find them.

6

The Little Bombshell

'So there you are!' The door opened and Mrs Elderfield appeared. When she saw Miranda her eyes popped out more than ever. 'And the little girl from over the wall! But this is very naughty of you, Eric. You know you're not supposed to play in the shed. Your father says it's dangerous.'

Eric didn't reply. He moved slightly to his left, masking the hole in the floorboard.

Mrs Elderfield sighed and turned to Miranda. 'I'm afraid I've forgotten your name, dear. Monica, wasn't it?'

'Miranda.'

'Oh, yes. Miranda. So now you two have met, after all?'

Miranda began to feel uneasy. It seemed almost as if Eric was ashamed of being discovered in her company. Also her thumb was hurting.

'Have you been playing hide-and-seek?' Mrs Elderfield asked with her bright, determined smile.

Eric scowled.

Miranda said, 'I've got a splinter in my thumb.'

'Oh, dear!' Mrs Elderfield's tone was sympathetic.

'You'd better come up to the house and let me get it out for you. I'm very good at getting splinters out. Aren't I, Eric?'

He muttered something under his breath and swung himself through the door and down the steps. He was back in his chair and turning it round before Mrs Elderfield and Miranda had time to catch up.

'He does like to be independent,' Mrs Elderfield murmured to Miranda as they followed him up the path. 'And of course it's very good for him to do as much as he can by himself.'

Miranda said nothing. She was afraid Eric might overhear.

When they reached the house Eric shot straight up a ramp that had been put down since Miranda's last visit, and in through the open french windows. 'Come inside,' Mrs Elderfield said. 'We're still in a muddle, I'm afraid, but at least we now have some chairs to sit on. Make yourself comfortable, dear.'

Miranda felt anything but comfortable. She perched on the edge of the sofa, aware that Eric was glaring at her from the other side of the room. She couldn't work out whether he was angry with her or with his mother.

Mrs Elderfield opened a padded silk box and took out a packet of needles. 'This may hurt a little,' she said, sitting beside Miranda. 'But I'll be as careful as I can. Hold out your thumb.'

It took all Miranda's self-control to let Mrs Elderfield probe around, loosening the skin around the splinter. At one point, when the needle dug sharply into her, she jumped.

'Keep still,' Mrs Elderfield said. 'You must be brave, like Eric is when he has to go into hospital for operations. He's very good, he never makes a fuss.'

Miranda glanced at Eric. He was scowling worse than ever.

'There, it's out!' Mrs Elderfield said triumphantly. She held up the splinter for Miranda to see. 'Quite a large one. Now, would you like some lemonade?'

Miranda was thirsty, but she wasn't sure that Eric wanted her to stay. She mumbled, 'It's getting late – '

'Oh, but you've plenty of time, surely? I expect you've just started your school holidays, like Eric.'

'Yes, I have. But – '

'Eric goes to a special school about fifty miles away, where we used to live, but now we've moved to Braddon he has to board there during the week and can only come home at weekends.' Mrs Elderfield stared hard at Miranda. 'It's not very nice for him, I'm afraid, especially as he doesn't know any children of his own age here yet.'

Miranda had an uneasy suspicion that Mrs Elderfield was secretly pleading with her to come and play with Eric. But was that what Eric wanted? Hardly, to judge by the expression on his face.

'I have to go,' she said firmly. 'Gran will be spitting mad if she finds I'm missing.'

'I must call on your grandmother,' Mrs Elderfield said. 'And introduce myself. After all, we're sort of neighbours . . .'

Miranda edged toward the french windows. She thought Mrs Elderfield might be in for a bit of a shock when she introduced herself to Gran.

'Do come again,' Mrs Elderfield called after her. 'Eric, where are your manners? Go and see Miranda out.'

Miranda pretended she hadn't heard. She went down the path to the wild part of the garden, but as she reached the wall she heard a mechanical squeaking behind her and the sound of Eric's sticks, pushing himself along.

'You don't need to see me out,' she said. 'I can get back okay by myself.'

'She wants you to come again.'

Miranda turned around to face him. 'I know that,' she said. 'But what about you?'

Eric didn't answer directly. Instead he smiled, as if he were enjoying some secret joke. 'You know why she wants you to come, don't you?'

'Because she thinks you might be lonely. Because you don't know any other kids around here. Because I just happen to have a grandmother who lives over the wall.'

'Not only that,' he said, still smiling. 'It's because you're a girl. She'd rather I played with girls than boys. Girls play nice, gentle games. They don't get into dangerous situations like boys do, because they don't want to risk getting hurt. They're not tough, like boys.'

Miranda had never been so insulted in her life. 'I'm tough,' she protested, sticking out her chin. 'I'm tougher than a lot of boys I know. Except Jason Fowler,' she added truthfully. 'He's the toughest boy in our class.'

'I'd like to meet him,' Eric said.

'No, you wouldn't. You'd hate him. He's a pig.'

Eric's eyes gleamed. 'Ask him over.'

'Are you mad? Your mother wouldn't even let him in the house.'

'I know.' He grinned. 'So ask him.'

'I'd sooner eat glass!' Miranda had had enough of this argument. She'd had enough of Eric – and his mother. She climbed the wall as toughly and dangerously as she could, and when she reached the top she sat astride, looking down on him. 'Why did you come to Braddon anyway, if your school's so far away?'

'Dad did a good business deal. We had to move.'

It sounded a bit like her and Mum, Miranda thought. They'd had to move because of a business deal too, only theirs hadn't been a good one and Dad had ended up in prison because of it. She muttered resentfully, 'I shan't come here again. It's boring, now it belongs to somebody. I liked it best when it was empty.'

'What about the hidden treasure?'

Miranda had forgotten about the treasure. She said with a shrug, 'It can stay hidden for all I care.'

'I'll go on looking for it by myself, then.'

'You do that.' She swung her leg over and jumped down into Gran's garden.

For a moment she stood still, listening. No sound came from the other side of the wall, no squeaking chair, no swishing of sticks. 'Earache?' she said.

No answer.

Miranda marched offendedly up the garden path.

'It was a stupid thing to say,' she complained to Mr

Wing later that evening. 'I don't care if he is in a wheelchair, it was still a stupid thing to say.'

Mr Wing ladled some leftover chicken chow mein into a foil container. 'Confucius says, people in wheelchairs can throw stones just as hard as anyone else.'

Miranda thought this was definitely one of Confucius's more confusing remarks. Perhaps that's why he was called Confucius? She said, 'Anyway, I don't want to ask Jason to come to Mount House. He might be unkind to Eric.'

'Perhaps that's what Eric is hoping for,' Mr Wing said, even more confusingly.

Before Miranda could ask him what he meant, the door opened and Mum came in, holding a brown envelope. 'I just went upstairs,' she said to Mr Wing, 'and found this little bombshell waiting for me. Did you get one as well?'

Mr Wing sighed. 'I'm afraid I did.'

Miranda peered at the envelope. There was just a name. 'Mrs Jones'. No address and no stamp, which meant that somebody must have delivered it by hand. 'Who's it from?' she asked.

'Our new landlord,' Mum says. 'He wants to redecorate our communal entrance and staircase – at our expense.' She asked Mr Wing, 'Will you be able to manage it?'

'Only by putting up my prices,' he said sadly.

'And I shall have to work overtime. Do you think we could appeal?'

Mr Wing shook his head. 'He's within his rights. It's in the lease.'

40

Miranda was silent as she climbed the stairs to the flat behind her mother. She was silent while she ate; and silent until it was time for bed.

'Don't let it worry you, pet,' Mum said, when she kissed her goodnight. 'We'll manage somehow.'

Miranda nodded.

But secretly she was thinking they could do better than manage; they could be rich, if only she could find the treasure. It wasn't a game any longer, it was the answer to all their problems. She needed Joseph Ebenezer Hardcastle's money – and she needed it soon!

7

Get-rich-quick

'Your Mrs Elderfield called round last night,' Gran told Miranda next day. 'Came to introduce herself.'

'She said she'd do that.' Miranda held out her hand to one of the cats. He ignored it and stalked off.

'Hoped we'd be good neighbours, she said.' Gran set aside the Patience cards and lit a cigarette. 'I told her old Joe Hardcastle and I had lived over the wall from each other for thirty odd years and barely exchanged a word. I've learned to get along without neighbours.'

Miranda wished she could have been a fly on the wall when Mrs Elderfield first met Gran. 'Did he always live alone?' she asked. 'Or did he have a family once?'

'He had a wife, but she died. About ten years ago, that must have been. No children.'

'So he didn't have anyone to spend his money on,' Miranda said thoughtfully. 'Poor man. Except he wasn't poor, was he? He was rich.'

'So the rumour goes.'

Miranda rested her elbows on the kitchen table and gazed into space. 'I wonder how rich, exactly. Do you think it could have been five hundred pounds?'

Gran gave a short, sharp laugh. 'Five thousand, more like. Maybe five million. How should I know?'

'Five million!' Miranda began to feel excited. 'I wonder if he kept it in notes? Five million pounds in notes would take up a lot of room. Or maybe it was in gold bars . . .'

'Or maybe he had a bonfire and burnt the lot.'

'Gold doesn't burn.'

'Melted it down, then.' Gran stubbed out her cigarette impatiently in a saucer. 'Why are you so interested in money all of a sudden? You're getting more like your father every day.'

'No, I'm not – '

'Get-rich-quick, that was your father all over. I always knew he'd end up in trouble.' She took another cigarette from the packet and struck a match.

Miranda stood up. She was angry inside but determined not to show it. 'I'm going out.'

'Out where?'

She didn't even bother to answer but stomped out of the kitchen, slamming the door behind her. Still angry, she walked down the garden path to the wall. Gran was wrong, she *must* be wrong, about Joseph Hardcastle melting down his treasure. It had to be there, hidden somewhere in the grounds of Mount House, it just *had* to be.

At the top of the wall she hesitated, looking for signs of movement below. She didn't want to meet Eric today, she wasn't in the mood. She wanted the garden to be Africa again, the way it used to be. A place where you could lose yourself in the jungle; and prove how tough you were by dealing with swamps and alligators and poisonous snakes. A place where you could be alone.

As soon as she was satisfied that the garden was empty, she dropped down into the undergrowth and made her way toward the shed. No, not the shed. The ruined temple. Here, where the jungle had closed over ancient tracks, guarding its secret, lay the answer to her questions. Somewhere, hidden beneath the floor of the temple, lay the treasure of Joseph Ebenezer Hardcastle . . .

She pushed open the door.

'Hello,' said Eric. 'I guessed it was you.'

She stared at him, speechless.

'You're wondering why you didn't see my chair,' he continued. 'That's because I hid it. I knew you'd come.'

'How could you possibly know?' she demanded. 'I didn't know myself till just this minute.'

He grinned. 'If you came to search for the treasure, you're wasting your time. I already did.' He stood back to show her that the floorboard with the hole had now been removed, and so had the one next to it, leaving a large gap. 'It isn't there.'

Miranda felt cheated. 'Are you sure?'

'Take a look yourself if you don't believe me.'

She knelt down and peered through the hole. The space beneath smelt of damp earth and rotting leaves. But he was right: there was no sign of a box or an old trunk, nothing large enough to contain five million pounds.

44

'Anyway, I've been thinking,' Eric went on. 'There's bits of the house I haven't managed to explore yet, because I can't get to them. And I reckon if the treasure's anywhere it must be in the cellar.'

Miranda stood up again. 'Why the cellar?'

'Because that's where the noises come from at night.' When he saw she was looking blank he added, 'You know, the ghost. Old Joseph Hardcastle, guarding his treasure. You must remember, it was you who told me about it.'

It was hard to tell from Eric's face whether he believed the story or not. He wasn't smiling, so perhaps he was serious about the ghost. Miranda felt both scared and excited at the same time. She must have been righter than she thought.

'Okay,' she said. 'Let's look in the cellar.'

'We'll have to wait until my mother goes out. She's going to the shops in a minute. She won't leave me in the garden, of course. I have to promise to stay in the house.'

'Why's that?'

Eric pulled a face. 'She thinks the house is safer. You'd better keep out of her sight. I'll go indoors and give you a signal when she's gone, like this . . .' He put two fingers in his mouth and gave a piercing whistle.

'That's loud,' Miranda said admiringly.

'My dad taught me.' Eric swung himself out of the shed and pulled his wheelchair out of the bushes.

When he'd gone Miranda sat on the steps to wait for his signal.

It seemed a long wait.

Never mind, she thought. It would serve Gran right if she were missing for several hours. She'd get worried then, and be sorry she'd said such unkind things about Dad. She might even call the police and they'd start a search. They'd put out a description of Miranda on CB radio and Mum would pick it up in the cab and rush round in a terrible state. And then Miranda would saunter in, very casually, wanting to know what all the fuss was about and Gran would break down in tears and say how sorry she was . . .

Eric's whistle interrupted her thoughts.

When she reached the house he was waiting by the french windows. 'We'll have to be quick,' he said. 'She won't be gone very long.'

'Okay. So where's the cellar?'

He jerked his head toward the hall. 'Follow me.'

8

Life's a Lemon

Miranda thought she had never seen anything so gloomy as the hall of Mount House, with its dark wood panelling and khaki-coloured paint.

'Whatever made your parents buy this place?' she asked.

'We got it cheap because it had been empty so long,' Eric replied. 'Besides, it has wide doorways.'

Miranda was puzzled by this, until she realised that wide doorways made it easier for Eric's wheelchair to get through.

'My dad plans to do it up himself, in his spare time,' Eric explained. 'That's how he makes his living, buying up places and doing them over and then selling them again.' He tried the handle of the cellar door. 'Just as I thought, it's locked. Doesn't matter, I know where she keeps the key.' He moved with the aid of his sticks to the far end of the passage, by the kitchen door.

Miranda followed him. 'What does your mother do?'

'Nothing. She says she already has a full-time job, looking after me.'

'My mum's a cab-driver.' She couldn't help a note of pride creeping into her voice.

'That's a strange sort of job for a woman.'

'No, it isn't. Not nowadays.'

Eric paused, looking at a bunch of keys suspended from a hook on the wall high above him. 'It's up there. You'll need to use the kitchen steps.'

She went into the kitchen and found the steps.

When she came back Eric asked, 'What about your father?'

Miranda stopped feeling proud. At first, when somebody asked about her father, she used to lie and say he was dead. But lying had made her uncomfortable; and anyway, she didn't mind so much now if people knew the truth. This was because, although she still wished he hadn't done what he did, she didn't hate him for it any more.

'He's in prison.'

Eric stared at her. 'Why, what did he do?'

'Stole some money from the people he worked for. But he gave himself up.' She made the steps secure and climbed on to them.

'Better not tell my mum,' Eric said. 'She wouldn't be so keen on you coming here if she knew. She only likes respectable people.'

'I – am – respectable!' Miranda protested, trying to reach the keys.

Eric gave a short laugh. 'She called round to see your grandmother last night.'

'Yes, I know . . .'

'She says she's weird.'

Miranda couldn't argue with this, expecially just now.

'She says she's the weirdest old woman she ever met,' Eric went on. 'And the house smells.'

This was also true. Miranda said, 'Gran's only a relation.' She made another attempt to reach the keys. 'Everybody has weird relations. Everybody in the world.'

'We don't.' Eric sounded almost regretful. 'What's the matter? Can't you get them?'

'They're too high. I shouldn't think anyone can reach them.'

'My dad can, when he's standing on the steps.'

'He must be a giant, then. Why did they put the hook up this high anyway?'

'To make sure I couldn't get at them with my stick.'

Miranda looked down at him suspiciously. 'How can you be sure the noises come from the cellar? If you're upstairs in bed . . .'

'I sleep downstairs,' Eric said. 'Dad's going to build a ground floor extension later, so I can have my own proper flat. For the time being I have to sleep in the breakfast room.'

Miranda was torn between envy for Eric having a whole flat to himself and natural scepticism about the ghost. She glanced at the cellar door. 'What's down there, anyway?'

'Old boxes, mostly. It's pretty damp, Dad says.'

Old boxes! She felt a shiver of excitement. 'What we need is a proper ladder. If we had a ladder I could reach the keys easily.'

'Well, we don't,' Eric said impatiently. 'You're too

short, that's the problem. I might have known you'd be useless.'

Miranda climbed down from the steps. 'If you think you can do any better,' she snapped, 'carry on.' She marched off in a huff.

Eric called after her, 'Where are you going?'

'Home.'

'But what about the treasure?'

'Stuff the treasure!'

Home! she thought ironically, making for the french windows. She wished she could go home, really home, to the flat above The Jade Dragon. To Mr Wing and chicken chow mein, instead of Gran's shepherd pie that always tasted as if it were made from cat mince. Which it probably was . . .

'Miranda!' Eric's voice was urgent. 'Can I come with you?'

She stopped. 'Come where?'

'Back to your Gran's. I want to meet her.'

She turned to stare at him. He stood in the doorway, his face white and tense. 'Why? You know she's weird.'

'I like weird people.'

Miranda shrugged. 'Okay, you can come if you want.'

'You'll have to put the steps back first, so Mum doesn't know what we've been doing.'

With a sigh she did as he ordered. When she returned she said, 'What if she comes back while you're round at Gran's? She'll have a heart attack if she finds you're missing.'

'I'll leave her a note.'

He scrawled a message on the back of an old envelope and put it on the mantelshelf. Then he eased himself into his wheelchair and propelled it through the french windows and down the ramp.

'Do you want me to push you?' Miranda offered.

'Don't be daft! I'd probably end up in the gutter.'

She followed him around the block until they arrived at Gran's house. At the front door he came to a halt and put on the brake. 'Steps,' he said. 'I'll have to get out.'

Miranda waited until he was propped up on his sticks before she rang the bell. While they waited she said, 'I warn you, you won't like her. Nobody does.'

Eric said nothing, but his eyes gleamed with interest.

Gran opened the door. A half-smoked cigarette dangled from her lips. When she saw Miranda she said, 'Oh, so it's you, Miss High-and-Mighty. Feeling peckish already?'

Miranda ignored the question. 'This is Earache. He lives at Mount House. He wanted to meet you.'

Gran looked at Eric. Eric looked at Gran.

Gran said, 'Saints alive, what is it with your family, always wanting to meet people? Well, I suppose you'd better come in.' She led the way into the kitchen.

Eric shot Miranda a triumphant grin as they followed her.

'Just made myself a cup of tea,' Gran said. 'No good offering you one, of course. All you kids drink is that fizzy stuff that rots your guts.'

'I like tea.' Eric bent to stroke one of the cats. It wound itself around his legs, purring. Gran, taking a stained mug down from the shelf, glanced at him.

'So what's wrong with you, then?' she demanded.

Miranda went cold all over. Gran wasn't just rude, she was tactless as well.

But Eric replied without hesitation. 'Spina bifida. I was born with a sort of lump on my spine.'

'Painful?' Gran enquired.

'Only when they operate. Mostly it's just boring, especially when people fuss.'

Gran pushed the mug across the table towards him. 'Life's a lemon,' she said. 'Looks juicy but tastes sour. And if you expect too much of it, it squirts in your eye.'

He nodded. 'I know that already.'

'Then you won't be disappointed.' She waved a hand at Miranda. 'Not like her. She's always being disappointed. But she'll learn, one day.'

Eric grinned. He bent to tickle the cat behind its ears.

Gran stubbed out her cigarette. 'You like cats. They can always tell.'

Eric said, 'My mum hates them.'

Gran smiled. 'I know.'

They laughed like conspirators.

He likes her, Miranda thought, amazed. But then Eric didn't have to spend every day with Gran the way she did. And he wasn't related to her either. He just saw her as a funny old character, like someone in a book.

She was relieved when he said he must go, before his mother got back.

9

The Outside World

'Gran says that Life's a lemon,' Miranda told her mother when they were driving home. 'Because it tastes sour and squirts in your eye. Do you think she's right?'

'In some ways, perhaps. But it's rather a gloomy view. I shouldn't take too much notice.'

'I don't.' Miranda stared out through the windscreen at the crowded streets. Being stuck with Gran all day was rather like being in prison, she decided, cut off from the outside world. She was beginning to understand how Dad must feel.

Eric must feel like a prisoner too, sometimes, shut up in Mount House.

Mum said, 'Gran hasn't had an easy life, you know. That's why she's inclined to be . . . well, bitter.'

Like lemons, Miranda thought.

Mum went on, 'She was only forty-five when my father died. It was a terrible shock to her. They used to fight a lot, but when he'd gone she missed him dreadfully. Of course she should have got herself a job straight away, that would have been the sensible thing, but she didn't. She just shut herself up in that house and kept cats.'

'And played Patience,' said Miranda.

'And smoked.' Mum sighed. 'Sometimes I think she's trying to smoke herself to death. She's not really old, you know. But she *thinks* old, that's the trouble. In fact she's thought herself old for the past twenty years.'

'If she was nicer to people,' Miranda said, 'she might make friends.'

'She doesn't want friends. She prefers to be alone, apart from her cats.'

Like Joseph Hardcastle, Miranda thought, except he didn't keep cats. Thinking of Joseph Hardcastle made her think of Mount House. And of Eric. She wasn't sure if she'd be seeing Eric again. He wasn't all that easy to get along with. Prickly, like Gran. In fact he reminded her of Gran in some ways. Perhaps that's why they'd liked each other so well, because they had things in common.

Mum turned into the supermarket car-park. 'I have to do some shopping,' she said. 'Do you want to come with me?'

'No, thanks,' Miranda said. She hated supermarkets. 'I'll wait here.'

'That's all right. As long as you don't change your mind and leave the cab unlocked.' Mum set off toward the entrance.

It was hot inside the cab. Miranda wound all the windows down as far as they would go. She twiddled the knobs on the radio, but she couldn't find any music, only a muffled voice giving messages to other cab drivers. She opened the glove compartment, hoping to find some chocolate, but there wasn't any.

She yawned.

There could be few more boring places in the world than a supermarket car-park. Especially a supermarket car-park in Braddon, which Dad had always called 'that dump'. She wished now she hadn't said she'd stay in the cab. She could have pushed the trolley round for Mum . . .

Something struck her hard on the side of her face. She looked down and saw a pellet of rolled-up paper lying in her lap. But where had it come from? There was nobody in sight, just rows and rows of parked cars.

Then she heard somebody laugh. A boy . . .

It came from about three cars away, but she still couldn't see anyone. Miranda opened the cab door and leaned out. 'Okay,' she said threateningly. 'Who's playing games?'

Another pellet stung her on the neck, this time from a different direction. Out of the corner of her eye she saw something move, and swung round just as a pair of bright yellow trainers disappeared behind a Ford Cortina. She'd have known those trainers anywhere.

'Jason Fowler!' she yelled.

Jason's head appeared, red hair sticking out at all angles, much untidier than it was ever allowed to be at school. He was wearing a Disneyworld T-shirt and a wicked grin. 'Hello, airhead.'

Furious, she got out of the cab and was just about to give chase when she heard a noise behind her. A very loud, rude noise, like someone blowing a raspberry. She swung round to see Tim Bosansky, Jason's best mate, waggling his ears at her. Now she didn't know which way to run.

But it was Jason who was her chief enemy. He was the biggest challenge. If she could only catch Jason it would prove how tough she was. She wished Eric was here to see her . . .

For the next few minutes they played a breathless game of tag around the cars. Except it wasn't really a game, it was deadly serious. Ignoring Tim Bosansky, Miranda concentrated on Jason. She got down on her hands and knees and peered under the cars, looking for the yellow trainers. There they were, away to her right. If she crept up on him from behind, she could take him by surprise.

She was almost upon him when suddenly a horn blared out and she swung round to see Tim Bosansky in the back of Mum's cab, waving in triumph. At that moment Jason pushed her from behind. When she felt herself falling she put out her hands to save herself, but the ground came up fast and hard. By the time she'd got to her feet again Jason was already racing across the car-park to join Tim. She limped after him and wrenched open the driver's door. 'Get out!'

'Why should we?' Jason demanded. 'This is a taxi, right? We want to be taken somewhere.'

'To the Leisure Centre,' said Tim. 'We're going for a swim.'

'We go for a swim every afternoon,' Jason added. 'We like to keep fit.'

'Unlike some people,' Tim said, looking pointedly

at Miranda, who was still panting from the chase. 'Come on, driver. We're in a hurry.'

'My mum'll be back in a minute.' She pushed the hair back from her hot face. 'She'll be furious when she finds you sitting in her cab.'

'I'd've thought she'd be pleased,' Jason said. 'She wants customers, doesn't she?'

'Not now. She's off duty.'

'Then she shouldn't drive around with a sign on top saying she's for hire.'

Miranda glared at him. She leaned over the back of the seat to mutter threateningly, 'If you don't get out I'll – I'll . . .'

'You'll what?' Jason's gooseberry-green eyes taunted her.

Tim opened the car door. 'Let's go, Jace.'

Jason looked at him in surprise. 'But – '

'Come *on*!' Tim was already half-way out.

Jason's gaze travelled past Miranda, through the windscreen. Suddenly he moved at the speed of light, tumbling out of the cab after Tim and bending low as they made a run for it.

Miranda turned to see her mother coming out of the supermarket, pushing a laden trolley. But she wasn't alone, she was talking to someone . . .

Mrs Crampton, their teacher! No wonder Jason and Tim had taken off at such speed. Miranda grinned to herself and crawled over into the passenger seat.

''Bye, Pam,' Mum said as she turned toward the cab.

''Bye, Anne.' Mrs Crampton waved to Miranda

through the windscreen. She pushed her trolley off to another part of the car-park.

Mum unloaded her shopping into the boot. When she got into the cab she said, 'Pam just told me something interesting.'

Miranda, realising that her arm was quite badly grazed, hastily covered it with her hand. 'What was that?' she enquired.

'Last day of term, apparently, you went to school in your pyjamas.'

Miranda had forgotten all about the pyjama episode. It seemed ages ago. She said wearily, 'It was Come-as-you-please Day.'

'So I understand. Pam Crampton thought it quite funny.' Mum started the engine. 'I'm not sure if I agree with her or not. I'll have to think about it.'

Miranda's arm was smarting quite badly now. As they drove out of the car-park she saw Jason and Tim Bosansky walking off down the street with rolled-up bathing towels under their arms. So they'd been speaking the truth about going to the Leisure Centre.

When she got home she asked Mr Wing if Confucius had ever said anything about Life being a lemon.

'I don't believe he did,' Mr Wing said. 'But if he had, it would probably have been along the lines of, If Life's a lemon then you'd better start squeezing.'

Miranda, deciding on a more practical approach, washed the car-park grit out of her arm.

10

Snakes and Ladders

'Pssst!'

Miranda was weeding a flower bed when she heard the noise. She looked round, thinking it must be one of the cats spitting at her in its usual unfriendly fashion. But there wasn't a cat in sight.

'Pssst!'

There it was again, coming from the top of the wall. Miranda stood up, shading her eyes. To her amazement she saw Eric's pale face looking down at her, his arms hooked over the wall. 'How did you get up there?' she demanded.

'Ladder.' He sounded breathless. 'Come on, we ought to get started, now we've got what we need.'

'What are you talking about? What do we need?'

'What, what, what?' he mimicked. 'The ladder, of course. Dad left it here last night, ready for the weekend. He brought it home from work. So now we can reach that key.'

Miranda's hopes began to rise. She climbed the wall and sat astride, looking down at the ladder. It was fairly short and made of metal. As soon as Eric started his descent Miranda said quickly, 'Wait, I'll hold it steady for you,' and jumped to the ground.

'Saints alive, you're worse than my mother!' He let himself down one rung at a time, bracing himself against the ladder with his knees. His arms must be very strong, Miranda thought, like a monkey's. And he had picked up that 'Saints alive' from Gran.

When he landed he moved back into his chair, which was parked nearby, and said, 'Okay, now bring it up to the house.'

He gave orders like a schoolteacher, Miranda thought resentfully. Nonetheless she picked up the ladder, which turned out to be lighter than she expected, and followed him. She had to concentrate hard on keeping it evenly balanced – so hard that when Eric's chair suddenly stopped she was taken by surprise and banged straight into it.

'Now what?' she demanded; then saw to her horror that he had fallen out and was lying on the path. She dropped the ladder and rushed at once to help him. 'What happened? Did you hurt yourself?'

'Path's uneven. Wheels turned.' He raised himself up into a sitting position. 'Don't fuss, it happens all the time. Just give me my sticks, will you?'

His sticks were clipped to the side of the chair. Miranda handed them to him and waited until he was sitting down again. She dared not say another word in case he should accuse her of fussing.

When they came within sight of the house he stopped again and said, 'I'd better make sure she's not around.'

'Your mother? But – '

'As long as she's in the kitchen she won't be able to see us. Stay here while I check.'

He disappeared. Miranda waited by the rhododendron bushes, holding the ladder. If anyone saw her, she thought, they might easily take her for a burglar.

When Eric returned he said, 'She's lining the larder shelves. That should keep her busy for a while. Bring it indoors.'

He'd gone again. With a sigh Miranda carried the ladder into the house.

Getting it through the french windows wasn't easy. Nor was manoeuvring it from the living-room into the hall, for all that Eric had said the doorways were wide. As Miranda turned, one end of the ladder caught a bag of golf clubs propped against the wall. They fell with a crash to the floor.

'Eric, are you all right?' Mrs Elderfield appeared in the kitchen doorway, her large blue eyes full of anxiety. They grew even larger when she saw Miranda. 'Oh hello, dear. What are you doing with that ladder?'

Miranda opened her mouth, but no explanation came out. She couldn't think of one.

Eric answered for her. 'She found it,' he said. 'Lying in the garden. She thought we might need it.'

'Oh, I see.' Mrs Elderfield sounded puzzled. 'Well, I don't think we really want it in the house, thank you very much. It'll be in the way.' Her blue gaze travelled to the golf bag. 'Is that what fell? Oh dear, your father will be – '

'I'll pick them up.' Eric swung his chair round.

'Don't be silly, I'll do it.' Mrs Elderfield got to the golf bag before him. 'I don't know why your father left it there. He should have known it would be a hazard. I'll put it in the cupboard.'

She opened a door in the side panelling of the stairs and thrust the bag out of sight. When she turned around she said brightly, 'I'm so glad you came, Monica. Perhaps you'd be kind enough to put the ladder back where you found it, and then you can both have a nice drink of lemonade.'

Miranda and Eric exchanged a look. Eric's said, Play along with her, it's the only way.

Miranda said in a meek voice, 'Sorry, Mrs Elderfield. I'll take it outside.'

'Thank you, dear.'

Miranda wasn't sure which was worse, being called 'dear' or 'Monica'. She carried the ladder into the garden and left it leaning against the wall; then returned to find Eric in the living-room.

'We'll have to wait till she goes out,' he muttered.

'When will that be?'

'I don't know. She – ' He broke off as his mother came in, carrying a tray.

'Here you are,' she said, setting it down on a table. 'Home-made, so much better for you than that awful fizzy stuff. And I've brought you some games.' From under her arm she took a couple of cardboard boxes and put them beside the tray. 'You can stay for a while, can't you, Monica?'

Miranda murmured she couldn't stay too long or

her grandmother would worry. Eric lifted the lid off the box of Snakes and Ladders. 'We'll play this,' he said.

'That's right, enjoy yourselves,' said Mrs Elderfield. 'I'll be upstairs if you need anything.'

When she'd gone Eric said gloomily, 'Snakes and ladders is about right. Soon as we start getting anywhere near those keys something happens and we end up back where we started.'

'Maybe the treasure isn't in the cellar anyway,' Miranda said. 'It could be hidden somewhere else in the house. There's all that panelling in the hall for a start. I'll bet if you twisted something . . . or pressed something . . . it would open a secret hiding place.'

Eric handed Miranda the dice. 'You have to throw a six to start.'

She threw the dice. It came up three. But it was no use, she couldn't get interested in Snakes and Ladders. There was too much at stake. 'Do you think your mother's gone upstairs yet?' she asked.

Eric threw a six first time. 'Probably.'

'Come on, then.' She jumped up from her seat and went into the hall.

The panelling was dark oak, decorated with bunches of grapes and vine leaves. The grapes looked invitingly like magic buttons, waiting to be pressed. All she had to do was find the right one.

Eric came to stand in the doorway. He watched in silence as she pressed and twisted and pushed and pulled. Every now and then she stopped to listen, hoping to hear a click or a whirring sound, like the mechanism of a safe, that would tell her if she was on the right track. But there was nothing.

She stood back, hands on her hips, and surveyed the staircase. Suddenly Eric asked, 'Where do the kids from your school hang out?'

'What do you mean, hang out?' Her gaze lighted on the large ball-shaped top of the newel post at the end of the banisters.

'Where do they go in the holidays?'

'Oh, all sorts of places.' She took hold of the wooden ball and gave it an experimental twist. 'Mostly the recreation ground, I suppose. Or the swimming pool at the Leisure Centre . . .'

The ball didn't move. She clutched it harder and tried again.

'I'd like to go there,' Eric said.

Surprise made her stop twisting. 'You can swim?'

'Of course I can swim! I bet I swim faster than you.'

'I bet you don't!' Miranda was proud of her swimming. Her father had taught her.

Eric's eyes gleamed. 'We can have a race.'

Miranda had a disturbing thought. If they went to the Leisure Centre they might bump into Tim and Jason. And although Eric seemed so keen to meet Jason, she still thought it wiser to keep them apart. She said discouragingly, 'I don't suppose your mother would let you.'

'She might, if I asked her.'

'I bet she won't.' Miranda seized the wooden ball once more and redoubled her efforts.

'Mum!' Eric yelled up the stairs.

Mrs Elderfield appeared on the landing above them. 'Eric? Is anything the matter?'

Miranda felt something give. *The wooden ball was turning!*

'Nothing's the matter,' Eric said. 'I only wanted to ask if you'd take me and Miranda swimming at the Leisure Centre.'

Mrs Elderfield looked doubtful. 'You know I hate water . . .'

'Please, Mum.'

'You'd better ask your father.' Her eyes widened. 'Monica, what on earth are you doing?'

Miranda held the wooden ball in her hands, like an outsize Malteser. It was no longer attached to the newel post. 'Sorry,' she mumbled, turning red. 'It just sort of came off in my hands.'

Eric burst out laughing.

11
Bang, Splash, Wallop!

On the following afternoon, as they were driving to the Leisure Centre, Eric said, 'You should have seen your face when that ball came off in your hands! Of course, I knew all along there wouldn't be a secret panel – '

'Sssh!' Miranda, sitting on the rear seat with Eric, shot a warning look at the back view of Mr Elderfield. This was the first time she had met Eric's father. Large and energetic, with a shiny bald head, he gave the impression of being a man constantly in a hurry. He certainly drove like one.

'Don't worry, he's not listening to us.' All the same, Eric lowered his voice. 'I already told you. The treasure has to be in the cellar, because that's where the ghost haunts. It stands to reason.'

Miranda wasn't sure that she believed Eric when he said he heard noises at night, especially as the ghost had been entirely her own invention. Nonetheless she was inclined to agree with him that the cellar was the most obvious place . . .

Without turning his head Mr Elderfield asked, 'Good at swimming, are you, Mandy?'

Miranda sighed. Couldn't anyone in this family get a person's name right? She answered politely, 'Pretty good, I think.' She was about to add that her father had taught her, but managed to stop herself in time. Best not to mention Dad, in case Mr Elderfield started asking awkward questions. If he held the same opinions as his wife, he might decide she wasn't respectable enough to go swimming with Eric.

'Eric's pretty good, too,' Mr Elderfield said. 'They swim a lot at that school he goes to. Got all sorts of facilities there, haven't they, son?'

Eric grunted and looked out of the car window.

'That's the trouble, you see, with going to a place like this Leisure Centre. No facilities for the disabled. Bit of a job getting him in and out of the pool.'

'They've got a hoist,' Miranda told him. 'I saw it being used last time I came. You sit on a chair and they lower you into the water. It looked a lot easier than having to jump in.'

'Is that so?' Mr Elderfield sounded surprised. 'Well, who'd have thought they'd be so go-ahead?'

He swung the car into the car-park at the Leisure Centre, took Eric's wheelchair from the boot, helped Eric into it and raced with him up the ramp and through the entrance. Miranda followed, feeling slightly breathless. In the foyer Mr Elderfield paid for all three of them and disappeared with Eric into the Men's changing-room. Miranda went into the Women's and put on her old navy-blue swimming costume. She wished she had a smart yellow two-piece like Chrissie's, but now Mum had to raise this extra money to have the stairs painted there seemed little hope of her getting one.

It was steamy warm inside the swimming pool area and very noisy. So far there was no sign of Jason Fowler, thank goodness. With any luck he and Tim Bosansky would decide to give it a miss this afternoon. Miranda jumped into the water and began doing her best butterfly, but when she was half-way up the pool she saw Eric being lowered into the water and stopped to watch.

He looked very tense as he sat on the chair attached to the hoist, his thin white legs dangling below his black swimming trunks. They must feel strange, Miranda thought, without the metal bits that usually supported them. Except, of course, that Eric probably couldn't feel them at all.

As soon as the hoist entered the water he slid off the chair and launched himself towards Miranda with a powerful breast stroke. When he reached her he said, 'Now we can have our race. Two lengths, starting at the deep end. Okay?'

'Okay,' she said.

As they swam to the start she noticed that he used only his arms to push himself through the water. In fact the top part of his body was so broad and muscly she wasn't at all surprised that he could swim so fast. She would have her work cut out to beat him.

Mr Elderfield jumped into the pool, also wearing black trunks. Considering that his head was so bald, his body was surprisingly hairy. Miranda thought he looked like a gorilla. 'Going to have a race?' he enquired. 'Good, I'll start you. Get set, backs to the side. Ready, steady, GO!'

It was neck-and-neck most of the way, but as they turned at the far end Eric was slightly in the lead. Miranda fought back hard, putting every ounce of strength she had into the second lap, and managed to touch the side about half a second before Eric.

'Miranda won, but only by a fingernail,' Mr Elderfield declared. 'I've just seen somebody I know over there. You kids be okay if I go and have a chat?'

They told him they would and he swam away from them with a splashy American crawl. 'I expect it's business,' Eric said. 'My mother says by the time he's finished buying up old run-down places he'll own half Braddon.' Without warning he dived under the water and seized Miranda's legs.

For a while they fooled around, then had another race. This time it was Eric who touched the side first, again only by a fingernail. He was a lot more fun to come swimming with than Chrissie, Miranda decided. Chrissie didn't really like getting wet and spent most of the time shivering on the edge of the pool. Perhaps in Australia, where it was warm, she might get to like it better . . .

BANG, SPLASH, WALLOP!

Taken by surprise, Miranda was momentarily submerged; and as soon as she bobbed up again and managed to clear the spray from her eyes there was a second splash, followed by loud laughter. She recognised the laughter at once. 'Jason Fowler!' she said angrily. 'And Tim Bosansky! You know dive-bombing isn't allowed.'

'So what?' Jason flicked back his wet red hair and trod water, grinning his most maddening grin. 'We come here more'n you do. We can do what we like.'

'Yeah, we come every day,' said Tim. 'First time we ever seen *you* here.'

'That's right.' Jason's grin grew even wider. 'I reckon you only came because we told you about it the other day.'

'Yeah,' said Tim. 'In the car-park, when you chased us.'

Jason pushed his face up close to hers. 'We don't like girls chasing us, Miranda Jones.'

Out of the corner of her eye she could see Eric floating. Floating and watching. She prayed that he would be sensible and keep his distance.

'Know what I think, Jace?' said Tim. 'I think she fancies you. That's why she keeps following you around.'

Jason's grin grew positively evil. 'You following me, Miranda?'

'No, I'm not!' She was so angry that she almost sank. 'If you must know, I can't stand the sight of you, you – you pig!'

'She doesn't mean it,' Tim said maddeningly.

'Yes, I do!' Miranda kicked out under the water, not caring which of them she hit. It was Jason who said, 'Ow!' and started thrashing around with his arms. One of them caught Miranda a glancing blow on the shoulder and she retaliated with a fierce push.

A stern voice from the side said, 'That's enough of that, young lady. You'd better come here.'

70

It was one of the attendants, a tall muscular boy who looked as if he didn't like being argued with. Miranda climbed out of the pool and had to endure a stern lecture on the proper way to behave in a swimming pool. It was so unfair. Jason and Tim had started it by dive-bombing, but she was the one to get caught. Behind her she could hear them sniggering with delight.

Well, at least Eric would know by now what Jason Fowler was really like, she thought with grim satisfaction.

But when she turned around, still smarting from the telling-off, she saw to her amazement that he was talking to Jason and Tim, as friendly as you please. Next moment they were all three swimming together down to the deep end; then having a race, two lengths, which Eric easily won. Boys! Miranda thought resentfully.

At that moment Mr Elderfield finished his business talk and came over to her. 'Had enough, Mandy? Right, we may as well call it a day. Eric? Eric, time to go, old son.'

The chair was lowered into the water. Eric, looking very reluctant, slid on to it and was hoisted out. Miranda, watching Jason and Tim, saw the astonishment on their faces and hid a smile. So they hadn't realised! Eric would be pleased, she thought.

He was more than pleased, he was jubilant on the drive home. 'That was ace!' he said. 'Best thing that's happened since we came to live in Braddon.'

Miranda couldn't help feeling a little hurt. She'd hoped that *she* might be the best thing that had

71

happened to Eric since he came to live in Braddon. The trouble was, she thought, that he seemed to like all the wrong people. First Gran, now Jason Fowler . . .

'Will you take me swimming again, Dad?' he asked.

Mr Elderfield promised he would, when he could find the time.

'Great! You'll come, Miranda, won't you?'

Miranda said she might, but privately she made up her mind never to go near the Leisure Centre again, much as she liked swimming. She couldn't bear to have Jason think she was chasing him. Even worse, chasing him because she *fancied* him. Ugh!

Anyway, from now on she was determined to concentrate on what mattered most, finding the treasure.

12
All Shut Up

'Next weekend I have two days off,' Mum said that evening.

'Mmm,' said Miranda, listening with only half her mind. The other half was trying to compose a poem for Eric, about swimming.

'So I thought I'd go down to see your father, and maybe stay overnight with Grandma and Grandad Jones. You can come with me, if you like.'

Miranda shook her head.

'Wouldn't you like to see your father?'

Miranda shook her head again. She still hadn't really got used to the idea of Dad being in prison. And it was only okay as long as she didn't have to see him there. That way she could pretend to herself that he'd just gone away for a while, for a sort of holiday.

'He'd love to see *you*,' Mum said.

'One day,' Miranda mumbled. 'Not yet.'

'Very well.' Mum sighed. 'But you realise this means you'll have to stay overnight with Gran?'

Miranda's first thought was Oh, no! Not that dark little bedroom she'd had to sleep in when they first came to Braddon, with large, hairy spiders lurking in the corners. But then she realised that this could be her big chance, her only chance perhaps, of going treasure hunting in Mount House. If she could somehow sneak out of Gran's house when it was dark . . .

'That's okay,' she said, keeping all expression out of her voice. 'I don't mind too much.'

On the following day Eric was waiting for her by the shed. When she told him that she'd be staying overnight at Gran's next weekend and planned to come treasure hunting he didn't look at all impressed. His mind seemed to be on other things, like hers when she was writing a poem.

'Oh, by the way,' she said, remembering, 'I brought you a present.' She took the creased-up sheet of paper out of her pocket and handed it to him.

She waited anxiously while he read the poem. He seemed to be having some difficulty. Maybe he wasn't a very good reader? Or maybe he didn't like it and was too polite to say so. She peered over his shoulder, to make sure it was as good as she'd thought it was.

> We went down the leshur senter
> Went to have a swimin race
> First to win wun was Miranda
> You shood have seen ole Earakes face!
>
> Sekon race was wun by Earake
> He swam farster than a wale.
> Tuched the side befor Miranda
> Wun it by a figernale

'Great, isn't it?' said Miranda, beaming.

'Not bad, except . . .' Eric hesitated. 'Don't they teach spelling at your school?'

Miranda's beam faded. ''Course they do. They teach everything. I never wrote poetry at my other school. If I hadn't come to Braddon I'd never have found out I was a poet. It was Mrs Crampton showed me how.' She snatched the poem out of Eric's hands. 'But if you don't like it . . .'

'I do like it,' he said quickly. 'I like it a lot. But it needs another verse.'

'Another verse?'

'About the third race. Between me and Jason.'

Miranda frowned. She'd forgotten about the third race, possibly because she hadn't been in it.

'I beat him easily,' Eric reminded her. 'He's not such a fast swimmer as you are.'

'I know that!' she said with scorn. 'Jason Fowler's not so wonderful at anything. Now you've met him you know.'

'I liked him, though. I'd like to be friends with him.'

This was hard to believe. She couldn't imagine why anyone would want to be friends with Jason. 'You wouldn't if you knew him properly,' she argued. 'He's a terrible bully. Yesterday – ' She stopped.

Yesterday, she'd been going to say, Jason hadn't realised that Eric normally went around in a wheelchair. He'd thought Eric was able-bodied, like him. That's why he'd treated him as just another boy. But now that he knew the truth . . .

The thought of what Jason might do to Eric if he ever got him in his power made her go shivery all over.

'Yesterday,' she finished, 'he just happened to be in a good mood. Next time it might be different. You'd better stay clear of him, that's my advice.'

Eric didn't argue, but his eyes held an obstinate gleam. 'Tell me about your school,' he said.

Miranda, thankful to change the subject, told him about Mrs Crampton and Chrissie and Maxine Dobbs, who was the most popular girl in 4C. But he wanted to know more than that. He asked questions about what lessons they did, and what maths book they studied and what games they played. And when she'd told him just about everything she could possibly think of he said, 'Let's go there.'

Miranda stared at him. 'Down to the school?'

'Yeah, why not?'

'But it's the holidays. It's all shut up.'

'Doesn't matter. I only want to look at it from the outside.' He swung himself into the wheelchair and started up the path. 'Come on.'

'It's a long way,' she warned as she followed him, but he took no notice.

Outside the french windows he paused to say, 'I'll tell my mother we're going round to your Gran's. She won't like it, but she won't try to stop us.'

'Okay.' Miranda waited while he went into the house. She felt a little uneasy. It was a big responsibility, taking Eric all that way in his wheelchair.

As it turned out there wasn't much taking to be

done. He was clever at finding lowered kerbs he could mount by himself and there were surprisingly few times that he needed Miranda's help. Going through the shopping centre he made 'peep-peeping' noises to warn dawdling pedestrians that he was about to overtake; and on their way through the park he let Miranda have a go in his chair, so that she could see for herself what it was like. It was more difficult to steer than she expected but quite good fun, just for a short ride. She would hate to be stuck in one for ever, though.

When they reached the school they stopped, and Eric got out of the chair to look over the wall. Braddon County Junior School wasn't old but it wasn't particularly new, either. It had several mobile classrooms and a large grey playground with a plane tree in the middle. Seeing it now, with holiday eyes, Miranda thought how dull and ordinary it looked. She said apologetically, 'It's much better in term-time, with all the kids running about.'

Eric was staring at the large blue noticeboard. 'What's he like?' he said, pointing with his stick at the line that read **Head Teacher: Mr A. Forester**.

'He's got a beard,' Miranda said. 'Eric, I just had a brilliant idea! If we go back along the High Street I can show you where I live.'

'Okay.' Eric got back into the chair. 'Let's go.'

When they reached The Jade Dragon Miranda didn't suggest they went up to the flat because the staircase was very narrow and she was afraid Eric might find it too difficult. Instead she took him to meet Mr Wing, who gave them a foil dish of fried squid to take away.

It was a special introductory free offer, he said, as Eric was new to the neighbourhood. But when they got outside again Eric said it wasn't likely to persuade his mother to use The Jade Dragon because she didn't approve of takeaways. So they stopped on the way home and ate the fried squid with their fingers, which was Miranda's idea of heaven.

Back at Mount House Mrs Elderfield said, 'You've been a long time. I was getting worried. What would you like for tea?'

'Nothing, thanks,' Eric said. 'We already had tea, round at Miranda's Gran's.'

Which made him, Miranda thought, almost as big a liar as she could be, on occasions.

He went on, 'Miranda's mum's going away next weekend . . .'

'On business,' Miranda put in hastily.

'. . . so can she come and stay with us Saturday night?'

Mrs Elderfield looked doubtful. 'Well, I don't know if . . .'

'Please,' said Eric.

'Oh, very well. Why not?' She smiled at Miranda. 'Yes, it would be lovely to have you.'

It seemed too good to be true. Miranda could have hugged Eric, if she hadn't known how much it would embarrass him. She decided instead to thank him by writing another verse for the poem, about the swimming race he'd had with Jason. It seemed the least she could do after the brilliant way he'd fixed it for her to spend a night at Mount House.

13

Dangerous Mission

'She's getting too grand now, to stay here with us,'
Gran told the purring cat crouched on her knee.
'Sooner spend the night with her fancy friends.'

'At least you won't have to make up a bed for me.'
Miranda fed bits of her cheese sandwich to the other
cats sitting watchfully at her feet. Tea-time at Gran's
was never very exciting; and anyway she wasn't
hungry.

In fact she'd been feeling queasy ever since Mum
dropped her off this morning on her way to the station.
It was obvious that Mum was disappointed in her for
not wanting to visit Dad; and although she had written
him a long letter, and got Mum to correct the spelling
and then written it out again, that still hadn't made it
right. And now Gran was making her feel even worse
by suggesting she only wanted to stay with the Elderfields because they were grand.

Well, she was wrong. And if Mum knew what a
dangerous mission Miranda was about to undertake in
order to solve their money problems, she might think
differently too.

'You just take care, that's all,' Gran said with a

sniff. 'Having grand friends can give you grand ideas and before you know it you're in trouble. Look what happened to your father.'

Miranda pushed back her chair and rose from the table. She couldn't bear it if Gran started attacking Dad, not today of all days. She said, in a very calm and grown-up voice, 'Mrs Elderfield told me I was welcome to arrive any time I liked. So I think I'll go round there now, if you don't mind.'

'Fine by me.' Gran puffed at her cigarette. 'Remember to brush your teeth before you go to bed. And mind your manners.'

Miranda ignored this last piece of advice. Gran was a fine one to talk about manners! As for brushing teeth, her own were so stained with nicotine they looked like little yellowing piano keys.

She picked up her overnight bag from the hall and took the long way round to Mount House. Overnight guests didn't climb walls: it wouldn't be dignified. Outside the large, shabby front door, which Mr Elderfield hadn't yet got around to painting, she felt suddenly nervous. The thought of what she had to do was quite alarming, when she stopped to think about it. Wait until dark and then creep through that big, gloomy house, looking for treasure that may or may not be guarded by a ghost . . .

She drew in her breath and rang the bell.

'Oh hello, dear,' Mrs Elderfield said when she opened the door. 'Nice and early, that's good. You and Eric can play a game before bedtime.'

Bedtime! Miranda was shocked. It wouldn't be her

bedtime for hours yet. As she followed Mrs Elderfield into the hall she noticed a strong smell of paint, which made her feel queasier than ever.

'Leave your bag in the hall. We'll take it up to your room later.' Mrs Elderfield sailed before her into the living-room. 'Eric, turn that television off now. Monica's arrived.'

Eric obediently switched off the television by remote control; and as soon as his mother had left the room he switched it on again. Miranda took the chair nearest to his and muttered, 'Where's the ladder?'

'Mmm?'

'The ladder. I'll need it tonight, for reaching the keys to the cellar. Is it still in the garden?'

'No, Dad's using it. He's decorating the landing.' Eric turned to look at her, suddenly more interested in what she was saying than in the TV screen. 'You really plan on going down there tonight?'

'You bet I do! I've got to find that treasure.'

Eric's eyes gleamed. 'We'll have to wait till they both go to bed.'

'What time is that?'

'Mum goes early, about ten. Dad could be anytime. He'll probably go on decorating for hours.'

That meant it would be ages yet before they could get started . . .

Miranda sprang impatiently to her feet. 'Why don't we go and help him? I'm good at painting walls.'

Eric sighed. 'She wouldn't let us.'

'We needn't ask her. We can sneak upstairs while she's not looking. Come on, Earache!'

Mrs Elderfield was in the kitchen. They could hear her singing dreamily to herself as they went across the hall. At the foot of the stairs Eric handed his sticks to Miranda and went up backwards, on his bottom.

They found Mr Elderfield high on the ladder, covering the dull khaki-coloured walls with a pale, creamy magnolia. He painted the way he did everything else, as if he were in a tearing hurry to finish. When Eric offered to help he seemed about to say no; but then Miranda pointed out it would be quicker with three of them working. 'You can do the top bits,' she told him. 'I'll do the middle and Eric the bottom. That way we'll get through it in half the time.'

Mr Elderfield clearly saw the sense in this. 'Okay,' he said. 'You're on. If you look in that cardboard box you'll find some old shirts you can use for overalls.'

Miranda chose a pink stripey one that came down to her knees. Eric put on an electric yellow one with a zigzag design in orange. No doubt about it, Mr Elderfield had a pretty flashy taste in shirts.

When they were ready he said, 'Eric, you can use the brush. Mandy, you any good with a roller?'

She assured him she was, although she'd never tried putting on paint with a roller before. Once she had started she found it was far easier than using a brush and twice as much fun. While she worked she memorised the shape of the landing so that she'd be able to find her way across it after dark. Luckily she'd had the sense to pack a torch in her overnight bag. Even so, carrying the ladder down the stairs was bound to be tricky.

'Ear – ache! Mir – and – a!' Mrs Elderfield's voice came fluting up from the hall. 'Where are you?'

'Here,' Eric called back. The streaks of paint on his face made him look like a Red Indian on the war-path.

'What on earth – ?' His mother arrived at the top of the stairs. 'Robert, how could you! Just look at the mess they're in.'

'They wanted to help.' Mr Elderfield looked a little sheepish. 'It's only emulsion. It'll soon wash off.'

She sighed. 'It's time they got ready for bed, anyway. Monica, you can use the bathroom first, as you're our guest.'

Miranda said meekly, 'I'll fetch my bag.'

As she went past, on her way down the stairs, Mrs Elderfield drew back her skirt to prevent it coming into contact with Miranda's paint-daubed person. She added, 'When you're ready, dear, put on your dressing-gown and come down to the kitchen. Eric always has a mug of hot milk before going to bed. It helps him sleep.'

Miranda hated hot milk, but she reminded herself that it was all in a good cause – the treasure – and did exactly as Mrs Elderfield had instructed. Scrubbed free of paint, more or less, she put on her dressing-gown over her panda pyjamas, and went downstairs.

The atmosphere in the kitchen seemed rather strained. Eric was in a silent mood – he had been in a silent mood all evening, even when he was painting – and Mrs Elderfield had gone dreamy again. In the end Miranda said the first thing that came into her head, which was, 'These are World Wide Fund for Nature pyjamas. I wore them to school on the last day of term.'

Mrs Elderfield looked at her and blinked. 'You went to school in your pyjamas?'

Miranda nodded. 'It was Come-As-You-Please.'

'Really? How interesting.'

Eric said abruptly, 'I want to go to Miranda's school.'

'Do you, dear?' Mrs Elderfield sounded vaguely amused. 'Well, I'm sure it's a very nice school, but it wouldn't really be suitable for you.'

Eric, pale-faced after his wash, tightened his lips.

'They wouldn't have the same facilities,' Mrs Elderfield went on. 'You're much better off where you are. I'm sure Miranda agrees with me.'

Oddly enough, Miranda did agree. The thought of Eric at Braddon County Juniors, being bullied by Jason at breaktime, filled her with horror. But she knew that Eric was hoping she would back him up, so instead of answering she pushed away the half-finished mug of milk and said, 'I think I'll go to bed now. I'm tired.'

'I expect you are, after all that painting.' Mrs Elderfield got to her feet and went to the door. 'Robert,' she called up the stairs to her husband, 'you'll have to stop. The children are just going to bed and you'll disturb them. Oh, and don't forget to bring that ladder downstairs. We don't want anyone tripping over it in the middle of the night.'

Miranda could hardly believe her luck. It was just beautiful the way everything was working out!

14

The Right Box

Miranda sat up in the big hard bed and shivered, even though it was August. The room seemed enormous compared with her bedroom at home. It had high ceilings, a threadbare rug on the floor and no lampshades. Mrs Elderfield had apologised for the lack of furniture, but said she was waiting until the room had been decorated. It certainly needed cheering up a bit, Miranda thought.

Reluctant to put out the light, she spent some time on Eric's poem. The third verse was giving her great difficulty, perhaps because she couldn't really put her heart into it. Jason Fowler didn't seem a proper subject for poetry, somehow. Eventually she heard Mrs Elderfield's light step on the stairs and hastily nipped out of bed to switch off the light. As she crawled back in again she thought how much darker it seemed than her room at home and how quiet. No streetlamps outside the window. No traffic. No Mum.

She didn't mean to let herself sleep, but she must have dozed a little, because the next thing she heard was Mr Elderfield coming out of the bathroom. The bedroom door slammed shut. Give them time to fall asleep, she thought, and then she must make her move.

The house was hushed, yet it seemed to be breathing. Perhaps it was her own breathing she could hear . . .

Or was it Joseph Hardcastle's?

Suddenly there was a noise on the landing, very slight, but enough to make her heart start thumping in her chest. She raised her head from the pillow to listen.

There it came again! A strange, slithering sound, followed by a scrabbling outside her door, as if something with fingernails was trying to tunnel its way in. In a panic she reached for the torch. As first she couldn't make it work, her fingers were so trembly; but when at last she managed to switch it on she saw that the door was open and Eric's face hung there, only about a foot off the floor.

'Oh!' Miranda gasped, sinking back. 'Oh, you gave me such a fright. I thought you were the ghost.'

'I didn't want to use my sticks.' He pulled himself further into the room. 'Mum and Dad are asleep. I heard Dad snoring. Are you ready?'

'Ye–es.' Now the moment had come, Miranda was beginning to wish she had never thought up the idea. But she couldn't let Eric see that she was scared. She added quickly, 'Yes, of course I am. But what about the ladder? Did your father – '

'It's downstairs. You'll be able to get the keys easily.'

'Oh. Great.' Miranda took a deep breath. She swung her legs off the high bed and slid to the floor.

As Eric started to go she said, 'Wait a minute,' and when he hesitated she hurried on, 'You know what you said earlier, about wanting to come to my school? Well, you wouldn't really like it, you know. It's nothing special.'

'No!' He sounded almost triumphant; and his eyes in the torchlight glittered. 'That's the whole point. It isn't special. Now, are you coming?'

She hadn't time to work out what he meant before she had to hurry after him, or be left behind.

Eric was already shuffling down the stairs on his bottom. Miranda followed him, gripping the torch, her heart beating so loudly she could hear it in her ears. At least the stairs didn't creak, but once or twice the banister did, when she gripped it too tightly.

As soon as they reached the hall Eric pointed wordlessly at the ladder lying against the wall. Miranda handed him her torch so that she could have both hands free, then bent to lift it as silently as she could. It made a slight metallic clang and they held their breath; but when no sound came from upstairs she carried it over to where the keys were hanging and propped it against the wall just beneath them.

This time reaching them was easy. Clutching the whole bunch in her hand she descended the ladder and held them out to Eric. 'Which one is it?' she whispered.

'I'm not sure. We'll have to try them.'

He turned to the cellar door and, with Miranda shining the torch on the lock, started with the ones that looked most likely to fit. The second key slid smoothly into the lock but wouldn't turn.

'Try harder,' Miranda urged. 'It's probably rusty.'

He tried again. This time the key did turn. He gripped the door handle and pulled it open. It gave directly on to a flight of narrow stone steps leading down into the darkness.

'Look, there's a light switch,' said Miranda. But when she pressed it nothing happened. Mr Elderfield must have been in too much of a hurry to put in a new bulb.

Eric stared at the steps. 'They're too steep,' he said.

Miranda could see from his face how sick he felt. Sick with frustration, because he knew how dangerous it would be for him even to try. 'You stay here and keep guard,' she said. 'I'll take the torch.'

He didn't even argue.

Miranda started down the steps, trying to look braver than she felt. The further she went the colder it seemed to get and she wished Eric had been able to come with her. It was easy to imagine a ghost living down here. If Joseph Ebenezer Hardcastle knew she was after his treasure . . .

When she reached the bottom the torchlight showed her a large, low-ceilinged room with thick stone walls. Miranda shivered. It smelled damp and mouldy, the sort of place where you might find frogs or toads or all sorts of slimy night-time creatures. But then she saw what the cellar contained and immediately forgot her fears.

Boxes!

Boxes of all shapes and sizes, mostly old cardboard cartons with names printed on them like 'Teacher's' and 'Haig'. If Joseph Hardcastle's ghost was lurking among them too bad, she thought. He couldn't put her off now. She was so near the treasure, it was almost within her grasp.

She picked her way across the cellar floor and sank on her knees beside the first box she came to. Her Wild Life pyjamas must be getting filthy, but that didn't matter. Nothing mattered except finding the right box, the one with all the money in it.

The first she looked into was filled with books, the second with old photographs. She glanced briefly at a black-and-white picture of a man and a woman sitting under a tree and thought that if that was Joseph Hardcastle he didn't look like a miser. Misers in books were usually thin and bad-tempered, but he looked fat and quite cheerful. But perhaps he hadn't been a miser when his wife was alive, it had only come over him later, when he was left on his own.

There was one box that looked different from the others, made of grey metal, the sort of box people usually keep in banks. Miranda's hopes rose instantly. This was the one, she felt certain. She tried to open it, and when she found it was locked she felt more certain than ever. She shone the torch around but there didn't seem to be a key. On the other hand the lock was rusty and weak: all she needed was something to force it open.

'Sssss!'

The noise came from behind her but she wouldn't be put off. 'Go away, Joseph Hardcastle,' she muttered. 'You can't stop me now.'

'*Sssss!*' The noise was insistent. She swung the torch beam up the steps and to her amazement saw Eric's face peering down at her.

'Earache! How did you – ?'

'Shut up and listen. You'd better give up. I just heard noises from Mum and Dad's room. If they come downstairs – '

'I can't give up now, I think I've found it. But I need something sharp to get the box open.'

Eric hesitated. Then he said, 'I'll get a knife from the kitchen. You'd better lend me the torch so I don't have to put the light on.'

She handed it up to him. 'Give me a whistle when you've got it. Don't try to come down the steps again.'

'It's okay. I've done it once and it wasn't so difficult.' He began to shuffle backwards up the steps on his bottom, leaving her in the dark.

She groped her way back to the box. This time she tried picking it up and was surprised to find how light it was, considering it was made of metal. So it must be notes inside, not coins. She shook it but could hear only a faint rustling. She tugged at the lid again, but the lock held. She would have to wait for Eric . . .

'And just what do you think you're playing at, young lady?'

Miranda swung round to find herself facing the cruel glare of her own torch. Behind it was a largish, darkish shape she could only guess at being Mr Elderfield's. She thought fast, faster than she'd ever thought in her life. Blinking hard, she murmured dazedly,

'Where are I? What am I doing here?'

'That's what I'd like to know! Come on up and you can give me an explanation.'

15
Yours Disgustedly

'Sleepwalking!' Mr Elderfield sounded grimly amused. 'Well, I've never heard of anyone sleepwalking up ladders before. Or unlocking cellar doors.' He turned to Eric. 'And I suppose you were trying to stop her?'

'Er – yes.' Eric flushed a dull red. He wasn't, Miranda thought sadly, such a good liar as she was after all.

They were gathered in Eric's bedroom. He was in bed, at his mother's insistence, and she sat beside him in a flowered dressing-gown, her long fair hair in a plait. Miranda stood stiffly, like the prisoner in the dock, while Mr Elderfield paced up and down in a short towelling robe that showed his hairy bare legs.

'It's such a shame.' Mrs Elderfield sounded depressed. 'I thought Monica would be an ideal friend for Eric to have and instead she's been leading him into all sorts of danger. He could so easily have fallen down those cellar steps . . .' She shuddered.

Miranda stared at her, fascinated. She had never seen a grown woman wearing a plait before. It made her look like someone out of an old-fashioned picture book.

'What I'd like to know,' Mr Elderfield said, still pacing, 'is what you were looking for? What on earth did you think you'd find down there – eh?' He stopped to glare at Miranda, his dark, square chin stuck out.

She gazed back at him blankly. She had to stick to her sleepwalking story, it was the only excuse she could think of.

His eyes narrowed. 'That box you were clutching – what was in it?'

'Box? What box?' Miranda murmured vaguely.

Mr Elderfield stared at her a moment longer; then swung round on his heel and strode from the room.

When he returned Miranda saw to her dismay that he was carrying the grey metal box. And when he began to prise open the lid with a pair of scissors, muttering, 'Maybe this will provide the answer,' she could hardly bear to watch. Any minute now Joseph Hardcastle's treasure would be exposed to all eyes and she could no longer claim it for her own.

The lock gave with a snap.

Miranda moved nearer. Just as she had thought, the box was full of paper. But it wasn't money . . .

'Letters,' said Mr Elderfield. 'Printed letters, cut out from a newspaper.' He read from the one that lay on top. ' "Dear Editor, I wish to complain about the level of noise pollution in this borough." Signed "Yours disgustedly, Joseph Hardcastle." And here's another. "Yours angrily" this time. Look, there's dozens of them.'

'Joseph Hardcastle,' Mrs Elderfield repeated. 'Surely that's the old man who used to live in this house. But why did he write so many letters?'

'He was a right tetchy old devil from all accounts. Must have spent his whole life complaining about something or other.' Mr Elderfield looked at Miranda. 'What I don't understand is why these letters were so important to you?'

She couldn't speak. Her throat was choked with disappointment and there was a dangerous stinging behind her eyes.

Eric answered for her. 'We thought it was treasure. Joseph Hardcastle was an old miser, her grandmother said so.'

'So he was, but I'm afraid he kept all his money in the bank. When he died it went to his nephew.' Mr Elderfield turned back to Miranda. 'So that's what you were looking for – money.'

Miranda felt so miserable that she didn't even bother to deny it. She had to sniff to stop herself from crying. 'I needed it for my mum,' she said, in case Mr Elderfield should think she was being greedy and meant to keep it all for herself. 'Our new landlord wants to paint our staircase and we can't afford to pay for it, so I thought – sniff – if I could find old Joseph Hardcastle's money – sniff – it would save Mum having to do overtime and – sniff – Mr Wing having to put his prices up.'

'That's Mr Wing who runs The Jade Dragon,' Eric put in. He cast a quick look at his mother. 'I had some fried squid there once. It was ace.'

But Mrs Elderfield wasn't even listening to him. She was too busy staring at her husband.

Mr Elderfield, however, was still staring at Miranda.

'You live in that little flat over the takeaway? In the High Street?'

Miranda nodded. She was so deep in misery now she thought she might as well get everything off her chest in one go, so she turned to Mrs Elderfield and confessed, 'And Mum isn't away on business. She's gone to see my father in prison. So you see I'm not really respectable and if you don't want me to be friends with Eric that's okay.'

'No, it's not,' Eric said sharply. 'It's not okay with me.'

His mother still didn't answer. She just went on staring at Mr Elderfield.

'I think,' he said abruptly, 'that it's time we all went back to bed.' He closed up Joseph Hardcastle's box and put it under his arm. 'We've had quite enough excitement for one night, if you ask me.'

Next morning Miranda came down for breakfast expecting the worst. She had hardly slept for wondering what the Elderfields would say now they'd had time to think things over. They had probably come to the conclusion that she was a Thoroughly Bad Person who must be kept away from Eric at all costs.

Instead, to her amazement, Mrs Elderfield greeted her as if nothing had happened. She offered to cook her bacon and eggs and fried bread; and when Miranda said no thanks, cereal would do fine, she insisted on giving her fruitjuice and yoghurt and toast and honey as well. Miranda couldn't make it out at all.

When eventually Mr Elderfield left the table and went upstairs to get on with his decorating, she muttered to Eric, 'Thanks for standing up for me last night.'

'That's okay.' He cast a wary look at his mother, who was at the sink, staring out of the window. 'You can pay me back, if you like.'

'All right. What do you want me to do?'

Instead of answering directly he raised his voice and said, 'Mum, can we go to the rec this morning?'

Mrs Elderfield turned round. 'Now, Eric. You know how I feel about the recreation ground. It's not a hygienic place for you to play, with all that dog dirt around.'

'But Miranda wants to go.' He appealed to her for support. 'Don't you?'

Taken aback, she could only say, 'Yes. Yes, okay.'

Mrs Elderfield said doubtfully, 'I suppose . . . Well, all right, but only for a little while.'

'About eleven,' Eric said. 'That would be a good time.'

His mother agreed that eleven would be fine. She seemed ready to agree with anything today.

When they were alone Eric said, 'It's not really the dog dirt she's worried about. It's the other kids. She doesn't want me to play with them.' He grinned gleefully at Miranda. 'I'm glad you came. This is turning out great!'

Miranda wasn't so sure. She had an uncomfortable suspicion that Eric was up to something. Why was he so anxious to go to the recreation ground at precisely eleven o'clock?

As soon as they arrived she had her answer. There, aimlessly kicking a football around the asphalt pitch, were Jason Fowler, Tim Bosansky and several other boys. Miranda was furious. She guessed at once that Eric had arranged to meet them there. He must have fixed it up at the swimming pool, after the race.

But that was before Jason found out that Eric normally went around in a wheelchair . . .

Which made it rather surprising that he had come at all. And even more surprising that he should stop playing football to wave at Eric and beckon him over.

'Oh, there's someone I know,' Eric said, deceptively casual. 'I'll just go and speak to him. Won't be long.'

'Oh, dear,' sighed Mrs Elderfield, looking after him anxiously as he wheeled himself away. She sank on to the nearest bench. 'I do hope he'll be all right.'

So did Miranda. She felt like rushing over to put herself between him and Jason, even if Jason did accuse her of chasing him. And supposing Eric fell out of his wheelchair again, as he had in the garden, but this time on to the hard ashphalt? But then she realised she was being just like Mrs Elderfield, wanting to stop him doing things in case he got hurt. So instead she made herself sit on the bench beside his mother to watch them play a game that seemed to be a combination of football and basketball and hockey.

After a while she saw to her relief that it was okay. It wasn't just that Jason and Tim were trying to be kind, they seemed genuinely to enjoy playing with Eric. They admired him when he did wheelies in his chair and applauded when he scored a goal.

'I think,' Miranda said, half to herself, 'it's going to be all right.'

'Yes,' Mrs Elderfield agreed. 'Yes, I rather think it is.'

After another pause Miranda suggested, 'You can go home now, if you like.'

'Do you think I should?'

'It might be best.'

'Very well.' Mrs Elderfield rose from the bench. 'But don't be too long, will you?'

Miranda promised they wouldn't and settled down to wait for Eric to finish his game.

When at last he did, and came over to her, he said, 'That was great. You should have joined in.'

'No, thanks. I don't much like games, only swimming.' She stood up. 'Earache, do you really want to come to my school? Because if you do I think I can fix it for you.'

He stared at her, his face still glowing from the exercise. 'How?'

'Come with me.'

16

Brilliant!

'This is Eric,' Miranda told Mr Forester. 'He wants to come to our school.'

Mr Forester, in a grey track-suit with scarlet trimmings, stood in the doorway of his house and stared at her.

'I found out where you lived from the telephone book,' she explained; and when he went on staring added, 'I'm Miranda Jones.' After all, it was the middle of the holidays and even head teachers could forget what their pupils looked like. 'I'm in Mrs Crampton's class. At least I was last term, but next term I'll be going up – '

'I know who you are, Miranda.' He glanced at Eric, waiting in his wheelchair. 'You'd better come in, both of you.'

Eric was out of his wheelchair in an instant. He swung himself over the doorstep on his sticks.

Mr Forester took them into his study. He told them to sit down, then asked Eric a lot of questions about the school he went to at the moment and why he wanted to go to Braddon County Juniors. Eric gave him some good, commonsense answers, Miranda thought. She felt proud of him.

'He's already met Jason Fowler,' she informed Mr Forester. 'And it's okay. They played football together.'

'Is that so?' He looked at her thoughtfully, then back at Eric. 'Well, it's perfectly possible. In fact we've already had someone in a wheelchair, the year before you came, Miranda. It means, of course, we'd need an extra member of staff, a helper who would look after Eric full-time . . .'

Eric said quickly. 'I don't need looking after.'

'I disagree. There are bound to be certain things you can't do, places you can't get, without help. But that can be arranged, provided the local authority agrees to the transfer. The question is, how do your parents feel about it?'

'I haven't asked them yet,' Eric said. 'But it'd be a lot easier for them than taking me fifty miles to school every week.'

'Well, that's your first hurdle. But if you're really determined – '

'I am.' Eric stuck out his jaw, looking just like his father.

'In that case you'd better ask them to come along and see me.' Mr Forester stood up. 'Goodbye, Eric. I hope we meet again soon.'

As they left the house Miranda found it hard to stop grinning. Outside Mr Forester's front gate she said triumphantly, 'There, I told you I could fix it!'

'It's not settled yet,' Eric reminded her. 'I have to talk my parents round first.'

'Would you like me to speak to them?' Miranda

offered. She felt so full of power that she was sure she could talk anybody round anything.

'No, thanks. I'd rather do it myself.'

Reluctantly, she agreed it might be for the best. As soon as they got back to Mount House she collected her overnight bag and thanked Mrs Elderfield for having her. Mrs Elderfield assured her it had been a pleasure. There was still something about all this pleasantness that puzzled Miranda, but she had so many other things on her mind she couldn't stop to think about it.

Soon after lunch Mum arrived, straight from the station. Miranda could hardly wait to say goodbye to Gran so that they could be alone in the taxicab; but as soon as they were she felt strangely tongue-tied. For some reason she found it impossible to ask the question she most wanted to ask, about Dad.

'Did you have a good time with Eric?' Mum enquired.

'Yes, thanks.'

'Anything exciting happen?'

'Well . . . yes, it did.' Miranda told her about going to see Mr Forester and Mum agreed it would be wonderful if Eric were allowed to go to Braddon County Juniors.

After that there was a little silence. Then Mum said, 'Grandad and Grandma Jones sent you their love.'

Miranda mumbled 'Thanks' and turned to stare out of the window.

'Your father was pleased with your letter. He read it twice.'

'Did he?' There was the answer to her question, but somehow it only made Miranda feel worse.

'He seemed better this time. More cheerful.'

She said in a low voice, 'I wish I'd come with you.'

'It would have been nice. Perhaps next time . . .'

'Next time,' Miranda promised.

Upstairs in the flat she was busy unpacking her Wild Life pyjamas – how on earth was she going to explain to Mum how the knees had got so dirty? – when she heard a ring at the doorbell, followed by Mr Wing's voice. 'I have important news,' he said; and Miranda went at once to find out what it was.

Mr Wing's round face looked serious, yet he seemed to be enjoying some kind of private joke. 'This morning,' he announced, 'I had a visit from our new landlord.'

Mum groaned. 'Don't tell me the cost has gone up.'

'No, it's gone down. Apparently he's decided the responsibility is mainly his, and he'll be asking us for only a small contribution.'

Mum stared at him. 'I don't believe it! What changed his mind?'

'Miranda did.' Mr Wing's eyes were now definitely laughing.

'It couldn't have been me,' Miranda said. 'I've never even met him.'

'Oh yes, you have. In fact you brought his son here only a few days ago. I gave you both a fried squid take-away.'

But that was Eric . . .

'Mr *Elderfield*?' Miranda's voice went squeaky with

amazement. 'You mean our new landlord is Mr *Elderfield*?'

It turned out this was exactly what Mr Wing meant. The next few minutes were spent sorting out how and why they hadn't realised it before; and they came to the conclusion it was because Miranda had never mentioned Eric's surname while neither Mum nor Mr Wing had told her the new landlord was called Elderfield. Miranda then had to explain how she had come to tell Mr Elderfield about their money problems, and how he'd gone very quiet. And how Mrs Elderfield had suddenly been terribly nice to her.

'Conscience,' said Mr Wing. 'They'd obviously not realised before how difficult it is for people like us to find a large sum of money in a hurry.'

'Mr Elderfield does everything in a hurry,' Miranda told them. 'I don't think he means to be unkind. He's really okay when you get to know him.'

Mr Wing nodded. 'Very few people are bad all through. As Confucius says, even a rotten apple can make good cider.'

Like Jason, Miranda thought.

'Miranda Jones,' Mum said slowly, 'you – are – brilliant. What are you?'

'Brilliant,' Miranda said modestly. And they hugged each other while Mr Wing looked on, smiling.

This made Miranda feel much better about herself, although she still wished she hadn't been such a coward about going to see Dad in prison. The very next day, when Gran started making snide remarks about him as usual, she tried hard not to lose her temper but instead counted to ten.

Gran was playing Patience on the kitchen table. She must have been playing Patience for years and years, Miranda thought, still counting, while on the other side of the wall Joseph Hardcastle had been writing all those letters of complaint to the local paper. Two lonely people, shut off from the outside world inside their houses. Perhaps, if they had spoken to each other occasionally, things might have been different.

When she reached ten she said firmly, 'Gran, I wish you'd stop being rude about Dad. I know he's in prison and I know you didn't ever like him very much, but he's still my dad and it makes me mad when you say those things about him. So I'd be glad if you'd just shut up about it in future – okay?'

Gran stopped shuffling the cards to stare at her. She opened and closed her mouth twice without actually saying anything; and when she did finally speak she said, 'Okay. You're right. Sorry,' and reached for a cigarette.

'And that's another thing,' Miranda said, encouraged by her success. 'You smoke too much, Gran. It isn't healthy.'

Gran glared at her, then stuck the cigarette in her mouth and lit it. 'Don't push your luck, miss,' she muttered.

Later that morning Miranda sat on the garden wall, looking down into Africa, and called softly, 'Ear – ache!'

She knew he was there, she could see the bushes shivering even though there was no wind; and seconds later his chair came bursting into the open. 'I've done it,' he said, and his eyes were brilliant as stars. 'I've talked them round.'

'Even your mother?' Miranda asked incredulously.

'Even her. At least, they've agreed to go and see Mr Forester. Dad says it won't be easy, though. There'll be a lot of forms to fill in and it's bound to take time. But it's going to be all right, I know it is.'

'Oh, Earache!' She swung both legs over the wall and jumped down. 'It'll be great, having you at Braddon. Here, look, I've finished the poem. The third verse. I wrote it last night.'

She handed it to him and waited anxiously while he read it.

> Then along came Jason Fowler
> He's pretty bad but not all through.
> He can't swim fast like Miranda
> So Eric won the last race too!

'What happened to your spelling?' asked Eric. 'You've got every word right.'

'I showed it to Mum,' Miranda admitted. 'She wrote it out for me to copy. But never mind the spelling, what do you think of the poem?'

He gave her a slow, admiring grin. 'If you must know,' he said, 'I think it's brilliant.'

Miranda glowed with pride. This was the second

time in two days that someone had called her brilliant. 'Actually,' she said, beaming back at him, 'I'm unique.'

Also in Puffin

ESIO TROT
Roald Dahl

Mr Hoppy is in love with Mrs Silver. But Mrs Silver has eyes only for Alfie, her pet tortoise. How can he ever compete with such a rival? He comes up with a bold plan to win his lady's love, involving some clever riddles and a whole army of tortoises. Will Mr Hoppy's patience be rewarded? And what's to become of Alfie?

A highly comic and unusual love story.

JUST FERRET
Gene Kemp

Owen Hardacre, otherwise known as Ferret, has been dragged around the country by his artist father and been to so many schools that he doesn't expect much from Cricklepit Combined School. But when he makes friends with Beany and Minty and gains the respect of Sir, things begin looking up . . . even the reading!

Meet Ferret, his friends *and* enemies in this fifth story of the pupils of Cricklepit Combined School.

DID YOU THINK I WOULD LEAVE YOU CRYING?
Moira Miller

This collection of sensitive and moving stories traces the effects of conflict and compassion across the years; the friendship, the heroism and the cruelty of war.

TALES FROM THE SHOP THAT NEVER SHUTS
Martin Waddell

McGlone lives at the Shop that Never Shuts, and Flash and Buster Cook are in McGlone's Gang with wee Biddy O'Hare. In these five highly entertaining stories the Gang dig for Viking treasure, are frightened that a sea monster has eaten Biddy, discover that McGlone needs glasses, look after the Shop that Never Shuts on their own, and give Biddy a birthday party.

VERA PRATT AND THE BALD HEAD
Brough Girling

When Wally Pratt and his fanatic mechanic mother enter the Motorbike and Sidecar Grand Prix, nothing is really as it seems. Vera's old enemy, Captain Smoothy-Smythe, is up to his old tricks and suddenly Wally is kidnapped. Rescue him? She can't do that yet, she's got to win the Grand Prix first. Two minutes to go and Vera finds herself the ideal partner – a headmaster with no hair!

CRUMMY MUMMY AND ME
Anne Fine

How would you feel if your mother had royal-blue hair and wore lavender fishnet tights? It's not easy for Minna being the only sensible one in the family, even though she's used to her mum's weird clothes and eccentric behaviour. But then the whole family are a bit unusual, and their exploits make very entertaining and enjoyable reading.